Matt Marinovich

THE WINTER GIRL

Matt Marinovich is the author of *Strange Skies* and lives in Brooklyn. He has taught fiction and nonfiction at Emerson College, Baruch College, and New York University. His writing has appeared in *McSweeney's Internet Tendency*, Esquire.com, *Salon, Quarterly West, Open City, The Barcelona Review, Mississippi Review,* and *Poets & Writers,* among other publications.

Praise for Matt Marinovich's

THE WINTER GIRL

"The slow, relaxed pace is perfect for building this almost ghostly, frightening tale. . . . As if stringed instruments are playing in the background, readers will feel dizzy with alarm and the feeling of foreboding that builds the thrills and chills perfectly."

—*Suspense Magazine*

"A psychological noir thriller. . . . One shocking surprise leads to the next, culminating in mayhem and revelations of twisted family secrets."

—*The Sacramento Bee*

"*The Winter Girl* is a dark and ever-darkening psychological thriller." —*Kirkus Reviews*

"Sharp and delightfully treacherous. . . . This is one of the leanest, meanest books I've read in a long, long time. I suspect Jim Thompson would've loved it. James M. Cain, too. And Patricia Highsmith. That's how great this book is." —Scott Smith,

New York Times bestselling author of *The Ruins* and *A Simple Plan*

"A sexy update of Hitchcock's *Rear Window*."

—*Travel + Leisure*

"The twists are clever and the pacing relentless."

—*Booklist*

"Unsettling but oh so fulfilling."

—*The Sag Harbor Express*

"Family secrets and marital transgressions weave a suspenseful Hitchcockian story of intrigue, mystery, and deceit." —*Library Journal*

"[*The Winter Girl*], like an impending winter storm, is filled with menace and the threat of destruction. . . . The story builds to a crescendo of murder and betrayal." —*The East Hampton Star*

"An engrossing, disquieting read."

—*Publishers Weekly*

"Watching this husband and wife steadily get in deeper and deeper is almost as thrilling as trespassing." —*BookPage*

"An unnerving and entertaining story."

—*Shelf Awareness*

ALSO BY MATT MARINOVICH

Strange Skies

THE
WINTER GIRL

THE WINTER GIRL

A Novel

Matt Marinovich

VINTAGE BOOKS
A Division of Penguin Random House LLC | New York

FIRST VINTAGE BOOKS EDITION, DECEMBER 2016

The Library of Congress has cataloged the Doubleday edition as follows:
Marinovich, Matt.
The winter girl : a novel / Matt Marinovich. — First edition.
pages ; cm
I. Title.
PS3613.A7488W56 2015 813'.6—dc23 2014040417

Vintage Books Trade Paperback ISBN: 978-1-101-87381-6
eBook ISBN: 978-0-385-53998-2

Book design by Maria Carella

www.vintagebooks.com

Printed in the United States of America
10 9 8 7 6 5 4 3 2 1

For Eve, Daphne, and Mato

THE
WINTER GIRL

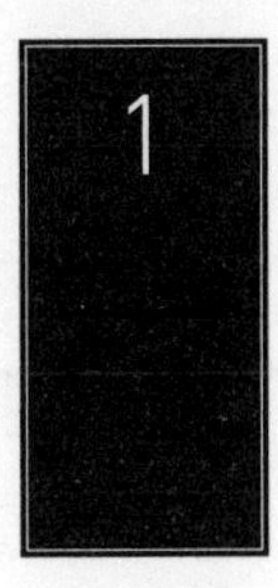

The two lights in the upstairs bedroom of the house next door were on a timer. I was certain of this.

They turned off at 11:00 p.m. every night, as if some ritualistic loner decided to go to bed at the exact same minute every evening. I remember I looked out our kitchen window one night and I said something to Elise about no one really living there.

It was early December and we were staying at her father's place in Shinnecock Hills, about halfway between Hampton Bays and Southampton. His house, like the others on Ocean View Road, faced the bay. In the distance, you could see that thin strip of sand where the most expensive houses were. Green and red lights blinked way out there at night, where the helicopters landed. That winter, I never saw one.

In the winter, hardly anybody was around. It was nice to see a distant light through the dark scrub pine.

We'd been staying there for three weeks, so that Elise could visit her father in the hospital during the day. His colon cancer had metastasized and she was forced to take a leave of absence at the office where she worked as a speech therapist. It would have been nice if we'd had some of her other family members to help us, but Elise's mother had passed away when she was a kid, and she heard from her younger brother only when he called to wish her a Merry Christmas from the Hamilton County jail in Ohio where he was serving a five-year sentence for distributing a controlled substance and burglary. Needless to say, it really pumped up the mood on Christmas Day when her phone rang and I could hear the recording: "You have a call from an inmate at the Hamilton County jail. If you choose to accept the call . . ."

Of course, she always accepted the call, closing the bedroom door so she could talk to him for a few minutes in private. Being the curious type, I always turned down the volume on the television until I could just make out what she was saying. Since I'd never met her brother, or even spoken to him, all I had to go on was Elise's half of the conversation. The only problem was that they spoke in a maddening sibling code. *V-Rex* I assumed was the nickname for her father. *The Hub* must have meant me. *Screech* was what she had nicknamed her profession for him. She always signed off with him in a loving, ironic voice that was one of my favorite things about her, mixing a perfect amount of affection and cruelty. *Love you, Greasebag,* she actually said once. He must have said something equally pithy, because she laughed out loud before he hung up. Then she composed herself behind the closed door as I slowly turned the volume up again, unable to ask her anything.

At night, Elise and I mostly watched television and avoided talking about how long it was taking her father to die. By early December, it was getting dark pretty early. By then, we had a routine down. I'd have dinner ready by the time I heard the wheels of our car on the short gravel driveway. Sometimes I'd watch Elise gather herself together in the Volvo, as if she were trying to put away what she'd seen in the hospital so that she could deal with me. The overhead light would flip on and I could see her reaching for things on the passenger seat. Once she gripped the steering wheel and pulled at it, as if she were going to tear it off. Then I saw her wiping the tears away with her sleeves, her mouth still gaping with grief. If you're wondering why I didn't run out there and comfort her, I don't have an exact answer. One of the reasons is that it had been going on for almost a year. He'd just gotten worse.

That's the terrible thing about watching a parent die. One day they look like they're ready to check out, and the next doctors might be talking about a five-year plan. They had assured us that it was a matter of months. Something in me was telling me that I had to pace myself.

The day she fell apart in the car was the first day I'd crept through the woods to take a look at the house next door. It was early in the afternoon, but the temperature had dropped below thirty and gray waves were sloshing in the bay. Hiding behind the crusty bark of a pine tree, I stood looking at the house's gray shingles, its bay windows, the fence around an empty pool that was shaped like a giant kidney bean. I stood there smiling, trying to look harmless, in case someone really did live there and was hiding behind a curtain, looking right back at me.

"It's empty," I said later. "I was right about the lights being on a timer."

I was standing over the sink, my glasses fogged by the rising steam from the pasta I'd dumped into the colander.

Elise was sitting at the table in the living room a, bunch of her father's bills in front of her, like a game of solitaire. A moment passed without her answering, but I was used to that. Our conversations had become satellite transmissions, like those far-flung reporters you see on TV, waiting for the delayed voice of an anchor.

"It's the off-season," she said, picking up one of Victor's bills. "Of course it's empty."

I felt a surge of blood warm the back of my neck. It had been my great accomplishment of the day, finding out the truth about that house. She was wearing her father's old Irish sweater. I walked up behind her and squeezed her shoulders, and noticed that she quickly put one of the bills behind another. I caught a glimpse of it just long enough to see that it was from PSEG, the electric company.

"Another late payment?" I said.

"Please don't start with that."

Every few weeks, she went through a pile of them and paid them with our money. She had assured me that her father would pay her back when he got out of the hospital, but the subject added only another layer of stress to our situation. I decided to let it go, for the good of the night.

"You want a massage?" I said.

She tore open another envelope. I started to knead her shoulder, and for a moment she leaned back and closed her eyes.

"Imagine if this house was ours," she said. "If we had a little space?"

"We can pretend," I said.

"It's not the same," she said, tapping my right hand to let me know the massage was over. She wanted to get back to looking over Victor's bills.

That's pretty much where we left it that night. We ate the pasta. We drank a bottle of wine. I can't remember what we watched on television. I know we didn't have sex. It was more or less like every other day that had preceded it for three weeks. In the back of my mind, I was wondering what kind of shape her father would be in when Elise showed up at the hospital in the morning.

I'm a photographer. I used to teach at the New School before they cut half the adjunct staff. In the fall, I ended up photographing Asian newlyweds in Prospect Park. It was a gig I got through an Asian student of mine. For three hundred bucks, I'd take fifty to sixty shots of the bride and groom, smiling at each other under some dying tree. It was always the same tree. An elm with a beautiful black bark that made the yellow leaves above seem even more unreal. I don't know why the work stopped. But by late October, I didn't get any more calls from Asian newlyweds, or even my Asian student. When I stopped by the New School to ask my old boss if he had any work, he asked me to walk with him as we talked. I thought that was odd since he had been sitting down when I walked into his office. We walked, he nodded his head, and he promised me he'd get in touch. Of course, he never did.

Elise is a pediatric speech therapist. She shares an office with another speech therapist in Park Slope, Brooklyn. On Mondays, Tuesdays, and Fridays, Elise makes seventy-five bucks an hour teaching little kids to say "car" instead of "tar." She has a real degree for this stuff, but one day, back when we were really in love, I pretended I was another speech therapist filling in for her. The parent brought her little girl in and I faked my way through a whole hour. Invented my own kind of speech therapy and probably set the kid back two years.

"You've got to open your mouth like this," I kept saying. "Like you're blowing a bubble."

I thought that sounded good. The little girl's mother sat watching us on the couch, and I could sort of see up her skirt. With Elise furtively listening outside the door, the whole situation became oddly arousing. Like I was skating on the surface of some real crime.

The funny thing about the day I pretended to be a speech therapist is that it also turned into the first real argument between me and Elise. I basically told her that she'd wasted seventy-five thousand dollars on a master's in speech and she told me I'd wasted ten years of my life pretending to be a photographer. We made up later that night, but looking back, I realize we never forgave each other. Part of each of us was always keeping an eye on the other from then on, even after we got married.

The day she heard her father was getting really sick, I drove the car to her office. I double-parked on President Street and ran into her office suite. It was the first time she'd let me back in since I'd pretended to be a speech therapist. It was a narrow office. I'm sure it still looks pretty much the same. A small desk. Sheetrock walls through which every loud telephone conversation of the lawyers next door can be heard. A thin beige wall-to-wall carpet. A thick wood door with frosted glass panels on either side.

It was late September when she got the news that her father's colon cancer had spread. I held her in my arms in the office. I said all the stuff any normal guy would say and I meant it. *So sad. I'm sorry, I'm sorry.* I would have added *He's a great guy,* but I couldn't force myself to spit that one out.

Elise's mother had left her father a long time ago. Her mother is Puerto Rican and her father's Caucasian. The truth is, he married his housekeeper. He was vaguely rich by then, making all his money in direct marketing. He had made a pile on the Hensu Knife, then sold his agency at the right time, just before the company diversified and went down the drain.

Needless to say, after years of abuse, his late wife or incarcerated son didn't make it to Southampton Hospital that day, weren't there to inhale the vague scent of urine in the private room. I was the one who kept on ferrying snacks back from the vending machine, buying newspapers he'd end up never reading, changing channels on the television above his bed as Elise held his chalky, dry hand.

I clipped his fucking nails.

Elise had fallen asleep halfway through doing them. Her father was asleep too. I watched the nail clipper slowly slip off the bedsheet and fall to the floor, and I sat watching it for a good long time as it got darker in the room, and *Arthur*, of all things, played on the television above his bed. After about ten minutes I leaned over and picked up the nail clipper and I resumed the job. It's odd clipping the nails of a sleeping man you vaguely detest. There were eight fingers that Elise hadn't finished, and by the time I got to his pinkie, he was awake, his dark blue eyes murkily looking at me.

"You're a manicurist now?" is what he said.

There was no point in trying to explain what I was doing, or how much his daughter loved him, or why I thought he was a hypocrite and a liar. Instead, I tossed the clipper on the table beside the bed and told Elise I was going to do some shopping in town. I stepped through the automatic doors of the emergency room and kept walking. I sat in our black Volvo S40 and turned on the radio and listened to 1010 WINS, the news anchor gently laying out the day's murders and a late report of a missing woman who was last seen leaving a bar with a registered sex offender.

I drove down Gin Lane into Southampton. There seemed to be a red bow or hanging strands of Christmas lights in the window of every store. Even the hardware store had gotten into the spirit, with a mechanical Santa waving his arm in the window. I was stopped at a light, trying to figure out why it seemed like something was missing, and then I realized what it was: people. There were only two people out on the street—an older couple who waved at me, mostly because they were concerned I might run them over when the light turned green. I waved back and continued driving down the empty street. Past a Saks Fifth Avenue, a clapboard church, the white picket fence of a small graveyard.

It was about two weeks before Christmas, and Elise was visiting her father in the hospital again, and I was standing on the frozen front lawn of his house, looking out at the bay. Peering through a set of old-fashioned binoculars. I scanned the inlet, where a duck blind bobbed on the opaque, wind-whipped waves. In the distance, on that spit of land where the most expensive houses are, a pool of golden sunlight was growing, carving itself into the sea until it blinded me just to look at it. I turned right and looked through the binoculars at the house next door. Its shingled, gabled roof. The sky reflected in its bay windows. The lounge chairs stacked up on one side of the pool. It was twice the size of Elise's father's house. Three chimneys. At least four balconies on which no one stood, admiring the view. There was a deer path that led from her father's property to the house next door, and I traded the binoculars for my digital camera and stole up to it again, looking through the lens as I walked toward the pool, as if being a photographer were the perfect excuse.

I let myself through the small gate that led to the pool deck, which was in terrible condition. I walked across it, certain that I would fall right through the wooden planks at any second. I looked down into the oblong concrete cavity, about fifty feet long, thirty feet wide, with brackish water at the bottom, the reflection of me holding my Nikon.

I walked around the house itself, touching the levers and handles of every door. They gave half an inch, but each one was locked. In what I supposed was the downstairs bedroom, a blind had been pulled almost all the way to the floor. Getting down on my hands and knees, I could see a low queen-size bed, a watercolor painting of an Indian squaw on the wall, and right in front of me, a phallic-looking cactus, drooping all the way out of its clay pot to get at the meager light that spilled onto the carpet.

I stood up again and moved quickly past the windows of the living room, noting a winding staircase and an assortment of incredibly green fake plants, including a ficus tree that had even somehow shed its fake leaves onto the painted wooden floor. There was a miniature Cleopatra statue on the glass coffee table.

I could see right into the kitchen. There was another bouquet of fake flowers on the counter, in a clay pot. There was a table right at the window, set for three people. There was a large porcelain pig wearing a chef's hat, and it was carrying a chalkboard, on which someone had neatly written THE BEST IS YET TO COME.

He's a little better," Elise said, when she got home from the hospital that day. I was tucking newspaper under three logs, building a fire. I watched the sports section burst into flame, an athlete's sideways touchdown catch incinerated. She was in the kitchen, and I could almost hear her thoughts as she slowly walked across the floor. *He hasn't made dinner. It's the least he could do.*

"That's fantastic," I said, stuffing more newspaper under the log, crumpling another sheet and getting it ready.

"What were you doing with the binoculars?" she said.

I winced a little, realizing I'd left them out.

"Looking at birds," I said.

Elise emerged from the kitchen with a skeptical look on her face. I turned toward her, my cheek warmed by the popping flames.

"Looking at birds?" she said, raising her eyebrow. She was wearing black cotton tights under a pleated gray skirt. She peeled off her black gloves, setting them carefully down on one of the pompous coffee-table books her father had probably never read. The log popped again and I pushed the grate back, sat down on the polished stonework next to the fire.

She looked at me with such a detached, sad expression that I had the dreaded feeling she had made a marital decision. I could see her mouth opening and I could already hear it. *I think we should get a divorce. We haven't been close for a long, long time.*

But that's not what she said.

"I'm sorry," she said. "This has been awful. I know you two don't even get along."

"No, no, no," I said. "That doesn't even matter now."

It did, but I was just happy we weren't getting divorced, on top of everything else.

"Do you want to fool around?" she said.

"Sure," I said, grabbing another sheet of newspaper, crumpling it. Trying to look useful and productive.

She walked up to me and leaned over, giving me a kiss on the top of my head, and I could feel all the cold she had brought with her from outside. A layer of it still hovering around her face.

By the time I finished perfecting the fire and found my way upstairs, she was lying crosswise on her father's bed, sound asleep. She'd managed to pull off her sweater and boots, but her black tights were still stretched halfway across her calves. I tugged them off and tossed them in a corner of the room, then I lifted her legs so that they lay comfortably on the bed. I found myself staring at her pink bra for a moment, and then I watched her stomach rise and fall. On the right side, about three inches below her breast, was an old appendectomy scar. She'd gone under the knife before she met me and had always been a little bit self-conscious about it. It had healed as well as it ever would, leaving behind a whitish, raised thread of extra skin. Before I turned off the light, I kissed her there, right on the scar, then on the valley of her stomach and once on her hip.

"I'm sleeping," she said, running her hand quickly through my hair.

"I know," I said, turning off the light.

Besides my steadily growing affair with the house next door, there were other disturbing developments that week in December. Whenever I came back from one of my expeditions to the house—I got as far as touching its windows, pictured myself scaling a drainpipe—her father's voice could be heard when I hit the play button on the answering machine.

"You son of a bitch," he said. "Pick up. I know you're there."

At first I thought he might be addressing an old colleague, mistakenly dialing his own number in a morphine haze. But there were many messages. Eight of them that particular day, his seething rage crackling on the phone's small speaker.

"Pick up."

"How does she let you touch her? You're a piece of shit."

"Pick up, scumbag. You fucking coward."

It went on like that till message seven, and I felt almost

reassured. I was hoping there was someone, somewhere he liked even less than me.

The eighth message cleared that up. He prefaced this one with my name and then told me that if he found me in his house he was going to drown me with his own two hands, right there in the bay. And he'd enjoy every minute of it.

"That's enough, now," a voice said, tearing the phone away from him.

When Elise came home that night, she shook her head before I could even tell her what I had heard.

"I was there," she said. "The nurse was too. Apparently, it's typical. Their thoughts become disordered."

"Actually," I said, "they sounded very orderly. He wants to drown me in the bay."

Elise arched her lip as if she would laugh, but then she must have remembered how crazy he looked when he said it, and the humor vanished.

"What's going on?" I said.

"I don't know," she said. She looked miserable as she stared down at the floor. Lines of mascara blotted under her eyes.

"Do you want to hear the messages?" I said, reaching toward the answering machine.

"No," she screamed. "Just turn off the phone. Why did you have to listen to them?"

She went upstairs and I thought the night would end there, but she was awake when I walked into the bedroom later. I could see glistening white dots where her eyes were.

She'd been crying in the dark.

I'd always suspected that she had an uncomfortable secret regarding her father. A friend of hers had hinted at it, years before, at a party. The friend had told me that she remembered one day in particular, when they were little girls. Elise's dad had pretended he was a monster and chased both of them around a playground. When he caught Elise, he whispered something in her ear and then gave her a long kiss on the neck.

That night, Elise told me about some of the other things he'd done to her, and then she told me she didn't want to talk about it anymore. It's not worth repeating any of it. It's sick and it's sad and a father who does that to his own child deserves a far worse death than being drowned in a bay.

I remember standing at the window at one point, watching the lights in the house next door. Even though we'd been married only four years, I thought we already knew each other's biggest secrets. But I told myself that one day, when she was ready, she'd tell me the rest, and I'd listen patiently, and then everything would be all right. I wouldn't force her to tell me the things that hurt her most just so I could move on. Otherwise, I'd be just as bullying as her father.

A steady wind was blowing across the bay, and the limbs of the pines on the hill erased the light for a few moments, then snapped back again. Precisely at 11:00 p.m., the lights went out. After that there was nothing much I could see in the darkness. Neither of us slept much that night.

In the morning, I waited to see what Elise would do. I listened to her shower. I listened to her brush her teeth and spit. I listened to her zip on her boots. I listened to her softly close the door, even though she must have known I was only pretending to be asleep, and then she left, once again, for the hospital.

That day, exhausted, I tugged on my sweatshirt and climbed up the deer path to the house next door. A coil of thorns sunk into my jeans and I leaned over and fished them out. I took another step and another coil fastened itself around my ankle. On that particular afternoon it seemed like the house was protecting itself. I made my way around a dark, pebbly mound of deer shit, and walked up the slight hill toward the pool. I knelt by the rusted pool heater and scanned the windows above me, the pale backs of chairs just visible through the kitchen window. The placemats just where they were the day before. That porcelain pig, still holding its optimistic sign.

After a few minutes, I stood up and walked around the fenced pool, up to the patio. Anyone could have seen me there, if they happened to be sitting on a boat in the bay. But there were no boats, just more gray waves rippling toward me, landing on the beach with a sweeping sound.

I remember that moment clearly, because I hadn't really done anything wrong yet. In fact, when I saw a door open on the balcony of a house across the road, I didn't wait to see who would come out. I ran back down the slope and found the deer path, tearing through the thorns that leaped toward me again.

I have an idea for a great photograph," I told Elise that night.

She was bent over a bowl of butternut squash soup I'd spent three hours making, tilting her spoon and watching the orange gruel slide off. She was wearing a Breast Cancer Awareness pin on her pullover. When you spend every day at Southampton Hospital, you get some freebies.

"The soup's a little thick," she said, eating another spoonful.

"I thought you liked it thick," I said.

"It's fine," she said, pushing the bowl a few inches away. "I'm just not hungry after the hospital. I can still smell his room."

She picked up the remote control and turned on the television. We watched *The Bachelorette.*

I never got around to telling her my great idea for a photograph that day, but I'll tell you. I was going to have her pose naked on the front steps of the empty pool of the house next door. I felt like it could be the beginning of a series. *Naked Wife Trespassing,* or something like that. As she sat watching television, I could imagine myself standing in the shallow end of that pool, my camera level with her naked kneecaps, goose pimples raised on her arms and legs. She would wrap her arms around her legs and squint at me slightly in the sunlight.

It would have been a great photograph. Even though I never snapped it, the image sticks in my mind, is always the same beautiful thing, just as real as the mundane facts of what really happened that night. We argued a little, lightly, over things we couldn't care less about. We poured ourselves more wine and sat silently through muted commercials.

I've never really taken my best photographs, but I can tell you what each one is:

A boy who fainted at the Fourth of July parade and was carried away by his father. The look of protectiveness, anxiety, and love in his father's eyes. The way the boy's sneakers dangled over his father's forearm.

Elise smiling at me from across the table, that day I brought her to meet my parents in Boston. A warm haze visible around her face, because we had been swimming in the ocean all day long and the salt was still drying in my eyes.

The curving road and the river of turning leaves above us, the net of shadows thrown over our laps, as we drove back from the Catskills one afternoon in October.

And then there are the ones I really would take a few days later. The ones that would change everything.

■

At 10:58, I stood by the bedroom window, watching the same lights in the same window of the house next door.

"Two minutes," I said, looking at the clock on the bedside table. Elise was flipping through *Elle Decor,* already in her nightgown.

"Two minutes to what?"

"Two minutes till those lights shut off automatically. That's real great security. Same time every night."

"I don't think they were counting on a guy who spends his evenings watching the house," she said, tossing the magazine on the nightstand.

"One minute and forty seconds," I said, standing closer to the window.

Elise turned the bedside lamp off.

"Don't you want to see this?" I said.

"I believe you," she said, turning on one side and pulling the blankets up to her neck.

At 11:00 p.m. on the dot, the lights in the window of the house next door shut off. My breath stretched an oval on the cold glass as I watched, and I wandered through a succession of dark, unknown rooms in my mind before finally returning to the one I was in. I took off my clothes and climbed into bed.

In the morning, I took the half-full coffee cup that Elise had left behind before going to the hospital, and I microwaved it until it was scorching. I turned on CNBC and aimlessly watched stock symbols crawl by, which reminded me of my own dwindling checking account. No matter how much pasta we ate, we were still going through our money. Her father hadn't paid for a thing. The phone rang, but I didn't pick it up. I listened to her father's scratchy voice on the answering machine.

"Where is she?" he demanded. "Where's my daughter?"

I listened to him hang up, involuntarily replying.

"She's on her way," I said out loud. "God knows why."

The phone rang again. It was Victor, just beginning to get himself worked up. His voice had a thick, clotted sound, an almost sexual tint to it, as if anger and arousal had crossed wires a long time back.

"You think you've got it made," he said. "You're in for a surprise. You're in for a very nice surprise when I die. You don't know anything, yet. You don't know what's going on right under your nose, do you?"

I didn't care about the colon cancer and the drug-addled state he was in. I'd had enough. I picked up the phone.

"Hi, Victor," I said, almost casually.

"Who is this?" he said, sounding meek and disappointed that I had dared to answer in real time.

"Your fucking son-in-law," I said.

I had a long list of things I was going to say to him. A surgically dismissive treatise of his entire life up to then and the awful things he had done to his daughter. I was going to pry it all open one last time and then slam it shut. I was going to close the case on him while he was still alive.

"It's my turn, Victor," is what I said first.

But I didn't get my turn. Victor hung up.

There's a note somewhere, deep in some landfill, that I wrote to myself that day. I remember the words exactly. It said:

STOP BEING YOUR SAME OLD SELF.

I remember writing those words, and then I remember being my same old self and crossing them out. I crumpled it up, threw it in the garbage, and pulled on my sweatshirt. The last place I wanted to be that day was in Victor's home. Surrounded by his mothballed sweaters and Dunlop tennis rackets and old shoes and pill bottles, and deeper in his closet, an old shotgun zipped up in a beige bag. One afternoon, crushingly bored, I had been tempted to pop two shells into it and bring down one of the endlessly gliding seagulls that always floated over the property. I stood there for a few minutes, raised the gun, but I didn't pull the trigger. I preferred my Nikon.

The house I was living in would never be mine. It was dry, with overgrown ghost grass leading to a deer path and another alien house. It was as if I were standing on a bridge that was being burned at both ends. I told myself that if her father would just die and we could get back to Park Slope, I'd feel settled again. But what roots did I really have there? I was a laid-off photographer of Asian newlyweds. It depressed me just remembering the hand signals I had to use, the frozen smile on my face, the frozen smiles on theirs. I might as well have been living on Mars.

To think that I had arrogantly put off having kids just so I could focus on photography. I told Elise we had plenty of time. We weren't even thirty yet. What would the child we might have had thought of that elm and the bridal parties I led across its scattered, bright yellow leaves? The worst decisions never let you go. They come circling back, even on the best days, to find you.

As I made my way up the deer path, camera in hand, attacked by the usual gangs of thorns, I tried to trace the lie of my talent. It might have started with my fifth-grade teacher, who, frustrated and a failure himself, had encouraged me and ordered me to always put art first. It might have started further back, when I laid out my drawings like stepping stones, so my mother would be forced to admire my one-hundredth version of a fire-breathing dragon when she came home.

As I stood on the patio of the house next door, the bay flashing beneath me, I pictured hurling my nine-hundred-dollar Nikon D70 as far as I could. It would crack through some branches below and disappear in the brush, along with a memory disc full of photographs the world could probably do without.

But the camera stayed strapped around my neck as I leaned up against the cold windows of the house, cupping my hands to eliminate the glare. Inside, in the enormous living room, I could see the staircase winding down. A low coffee table. The fake ficus, its leaves blown across a tan, wooden floor. A stack of coffee-table books tilting behind a chair, the top one blandly titled *Impressionism*. It looked a little like a stage set. Later, I would sometimes think of everything that happened in that house as a kind of play. A performance that neither of us knew we were capable of.

I tried the usual door, pressing down that half-inch before I felt the lock. I sensed my curiosity change. I was becoming impatient. I wanted to find a way into the house that was much more subtle than breaking a window. I tried each door on the bay-facing side and then I walked toward the driveway, stopping to press my face against another window. The master bedroom. Three photographs on a dresser: a plain-faced middle-aged man and a blond wife, but through the screen I could barely make out their faces. Some photo with a horse in it. One on a beach. I cupped my hands again and peered in another window. A pink Jacuzzi bathtub. Bath-oil beads in a jar and designer shampoos. A terry-cloth robe hanging on the door.

Under a pine tree about twenty yards away, more lawn furniture had been piled up, the plastic covered with a fine layer of dead pine needles. There was a Weber grill, uncovered, with a pair of rusted tongs hanging from its side. There was something about trespassing that aroused me in a slightly disturbing way.

I walked around the front of the house, my feet crunching on the blue gravel, and suddenly heard a noise in the dry leaves. I immediately thought someone was watching me, but it was a deer, bounding away. I took a deep breath and continued walking toward the front door, wondering what I would have said if I had seen a person there instead.

The clouds, which had been thick for two days, split

enough to momentarily whiten the driveway, and the sun briefly flashed in the windows above me. I waited a moment, and then I walked up to the front porch steps, surprised that the iron railing was slightly loose. I tried the front door and was actually half turning to walk away when I realized it was unlocked.

I don't know why I did this. But I shook my head as I walked into the house for the first time. If someone were watching me, they might think I was silently cursing myself for forgetting my keys.

Once inside, I carefully closed the door, my heart knocking against my chest, blood fizzling in my ears.

"Hello," I actually said, panting. "Is anybody home?"

My first visit didn't last more than five minutes. I felt as if, at any second, someone might appear behind me and ask me what the fuck I was doing. I think everybody should have a what-the-fuck-are-you-doing? moment in their life. I highly recommend it. All my overrefined worries dropped away as I stepped into the living room.

I had not been invited into this house, so at first I stood there, like a deer, waiting to hear if there was anyone there but me. There wasn't a sound. Not inside, or outside, only the bright afternoon light shifting slightly over the furniture in the living room. For days I had been wanting to touch these objects, and now I did. I walked slowly across the living room floor—it was a parquet floor, painted white—until I reached the glass coffee table where the small black statue of Cleopatra sat. From the window, I hadn't been able to see her upturned breasts and wide, hollow eyes. I leaned over and touched the top of her wooden head, smiling to myself.

Above the fireplace, there was a white orchid. I rubbed a

petal between my fingers. From the outside, I had known it was fake, but now I felt the slightly coarse fabric between my fingers.

I trailed my index finger across the dust of a coffee-table book titled *Rodin* that had been left on the seat of an upholstered armchair. I picked up the heavy book and sat down, listening to the fancy frame of the chair creak underneath my weight. I crossed my legs and turned a few stiff pages, as if my being there was the most natural thing in the world. I noticed a faint burning smell coming from somewhere, not entirely pleasant, like singed rubber or plastic.

I stood up and passed through the dining room, rubbing my thumb against the beveled edge of the glass table. A small platoon of tacky, flowery plates hung on a wall. I suddenly had the urge to take one and send it flying into a wall, a small act of destruction I'd never contemplate in Victor's house.

A handful of different-sized crystal decanters sat on a sideboard, all filled with amber-colored cordials. I lifted out a crystal stopper and poured the darkest one into a dusty snifter, swirled it around and sniffed it. I took a small sip, felt the warm alcohol slide under my tongue.

Then I heard a noise, upstairs, and I swear, for three or four seconds, my heart didn't even beat. I didn't even swallow the alcohol left in my mouth. The small snifter stayed frozen in the air, as if I were toasting someone. I pictured some man coming down the winding staircase, tying some silk belt around a silk robe as he made his way toward me.

I think I waited a minute, but there were no more sounds. I decided not to push my luck. I told myself that this was far enough. I could always come back.

I had entered mumbling to myself, still pretending I was someone else, but I left without saying a word. I just closed the door and calmly walked away. Looking back, I realize I hadn't changed yet. It was too early for that. But there was something natural about the way I walked away. Upright, unhurried, aware. It's the way intruders walk, and I swear, you either have it or you don't. It can't be taught.

“The front door was open,” I said to Elise, pouring her another glass of wine. “I let myself in.”

She tilted her head back as she sipped the wine, her dark eyes fixed on me.

“You’re going to get arrested,” she said. “And I’m not going to bail you out.”

“It’s harmless fun,” I said, reaching out to touch her hand. She pulled it away.

“It’s our next-door neighbor,” she said. “Normal people don’t invade the houses of their next-door neighbors.”

“There’s no one living there. They won’t be back till the summer.”

She twisted her fingers around the stem of the wineglass and shook her head slowly, but there was a smile on her face. That’s when I knew I could show her around the house next door.

We got drunk that night, for the first time in weeks. We pretended our trespassing was just a game. I put on her father’s old duck-hunting outfit, the camouflaged canvas scratching against my elbows. I pulled on a pair of rubber boots. Elise changed into a black turtleneck sweater, found a pair of her old L.L.Bean galoshes and a black pair of jeans she swore she'd never wear again. It was pitch black outside and raining. An insistent, tapping precipitation that hadn't bothered either of us all night, until we got outside.

"I need a hat," she said.

"Fuck the hat," I said, handing her the bottle of wine. She took a sip and handed it to me, the last of her father's Malbec sloshing in the bottle. Intermittently turning on a flashlight, I led her down the driveway, over the wooden fence, down the deer path. Halfway there, we found ourselves in a small gully, mats of wet leaves attached to our boots by then, like snowshoes.

"I'm going home," she said, catching my elbow as she nearly slipped.

"Come on," I said. "It's two steps away."

I felt like we were back in college, stumbling around in the woods after taking two hits of Ecstasy. I held her hand and pulled her toward me the same way. Three weeks of feeling like a grim, aging couple just fell away. I kissed her and warned her about the thorns. I felt them encircling our legs, but the moisture rendered the points harmless. We just kicked them away and they made useless snatching sounds and then we were in the clearing, listening to rain patter on the deck of the pool.

"It's empty," I said. "They didn't even bother to cover it."

If someone had been able to see us from the window of that house, I think we would have looked like mischievous children, slightly crouched, holding hands. I wonder how we must have looked as we crept around the pool, as I shushed Elise when she started laughing. Our silhouettes must have been clearly distinct on the patio, even in the rain.

"Where's the wine bottle?" she said.

"I don't know," I said, pressing the palm of my hand down so that she'd crouch next to me. "I thought you had it."

"What are we doing?" she said, as she knelt down next to me on the slick patio, rain beating on our shoulders. "Praying?"

"We're surveilling," I said, wiping moisture off my glasses with my sleeve. I put them back on and saw only a vague white haze where the light was. "We have to go around the side."

Still crouching, we crept around the side of the house, past the outdoor grill and the cadaverous mound of lawn furniture. Our footsteps could barely be heard on the wet gravel. My hand made no sound as it grasped the lever of the front door and pushed it open. Elise followed me in and I closed it behind us.

We must have looked pretty idiotic, standing there dripping all over the place. Me in my oversized camouflage duck-hunting jacket and Elise looking like a B-movie spy in her sopping turtleneck. The recessed lights in the living room were on, throwing a faint light on the coffee table and the striped chair I had sat in earlier that day.

"This is creepy," Elise said, but she looked delighted.

We walked past the wall of plates and the dining room table.

"Nice," Elise said sarcastically, touching the wooden beak of one of the carved birds that sat on the table. She slipped her hand inside my jacket, pulling me a little closer to her. I could feel her cold hand on my waist.

"You want to fuck me right now?" she said. "On this table."

"Let me show you the rest of the house first," I said, taking her hand.

I walked into the kitchen, flipped on the light, and watched the white tiles and marble counter come to life in freeze frames. I stared out the window over the sink and touched a plastic Baggie that had been draped over the lever.

"Weird," I said. "Maybe someone's worried about fingerprints."

Elise ran her hand over the countertop, rubbed some dust between her fingers.

"It's Corian," Elise said distastefully. "From Home Depot."

I opened the refrigerator. There was a box of baking soda in the back; that was it. No, that's not correct. There was a yellow onion in the sliding drawer. I pulled the drawer out and held up the withered onion. Judging by its inner collapse, I estimated that it had been there for at least six months.

"The best is yet to come," Elise said, reading what was written on the porcelain pig's chalkboard.

When you share a secret with someone, the mystery is cut by half. But I still felt excited to be there.

I deposited the withered onion back in its vegetable drawer and closed the refrigerator door. There was a dusty Panasonic handheld phone on the wall that had twenty-four messages.

I pressed the playback button.

We listened to the detached voices of friends and businessmen, all looking for a couple who sounded like they were doing their best to avoid everyone.

"Swainy," a chummy-sounding man said. "Where the hell are you this summer? Give me a call. Let's do dinner at the Peconic Grill."

"Mr. Swain," a professional-sounding female said. "This is Samantha at Southampton Catering. We still haven't received payment for the event last August. Please call me immediately."

There were a few more calls like that: someone from a lawn-care company calling twice about a bill that had never been paid, a pool-cleaning person warning that they would not proceed with the acid-washing of the pool if Mr. Swain did not remit payment. There were a few more personal calls as well.

"Martha," a croaky-sounding woman said. "Pilates just isn't the same without you. I'm not going until I hear from you. If I get fat and die it's going to be your fault."

"Swainy," a more agitated-sounding chummy guy said. "It's Bill again. You better be dead. Because it's almost September and I still haven't heard from you. This is your last chance to meet us at the Peconic Grill. The oysters are on me."

Other confused friends left similar messages, wondering why the Swains had never gotten back to them. There was the sense of a whole summer passing without Mr. Swain or his wife making an appearance. And then it was winter, because East End Pools was calling again.

"Mr. Swain," a tired-sounding man said, as if he were moving down a list of the most derelict and hopeless customers. "We cannot drain your pool if you don't pay your current balance. I would say there is a one hundred percent chance that the concrete foundation cracks if it isn't drained properly."

Elise moved closer to me and reached out toward the phone, her finger an inch from the delete button. She was just about to press it when we heard a different kind of message.

"Carmelita?" a man said. His voice sounded a bit bland, as if he weren't sure he had called the right number. I could hear him breathing and the faint sound of a television playing in the background. Then he hung up.

"He sounds familiar," I said.

"Let's not freak ourselves out," Elise said, reaching for the stop button on the machine. She hesitated and didn't push it down. Another message from the same man.

"Carmelita," the man said. "I'm worried about you. I know you're listening. I know you're standing there."

It was Victor. Beyond a doubt. And when I looked up at my wife, I knew that she realized it was her father too.

"It's your dad," I said. "That's his voice."

"Are you crazy?" she said, listening to the sound of the television in the background. If it was Victor on the phone, he was still waiting for this woman named Carmelita to pick up the receiver. I imagined her, standing there just as we were, listening to his gravelly, sleep-deprived voice.

"Come on, Elise," I said, waiting for her anxious expression to soften. Of all the people in the world, she'd be the one able to identify her father's voice. But instead of admitting it, she did something strange. She tried to hit delete. All before we could hear another message. I caught her wrist and pulled it back, stopping her.

"It's not him," she shouted at me. "There are a thousand old guys who sound like that. You're just trying to mess with my head. We shouldn't even be here."

"Okay," I said, relenting. The excitement of exploring the house further would definitely have to take precedence over an old answering machine. "Let's not ruin the fun."

My voice had turned to a playful whisper again, and Elise finally allowed herself a quick smile. For a moment, it felt like all that had built up between us had vanished. I knew that resentment would return as soon as things felt ordinary again, but I had this feeling that as long as we snuck around this house, we might stop finding ways out of the marriage. You need each other more when you have no idea what's going to happen next.

There was no denying the thrill of it. The faint smell of dust in the air, as if the windows hadn't been opened for months. The cold air making the ordinary kitchen light above us seem even more surreal. I felt like a suburban astronaut, exploring an abandoned home in which the crew had gone missing.

I watched her walk past the counter, swabbing up some dust with her index finger. She tried the door in the corner.

"Probably leads down to the basement," she said, watching me come to her with a lascivious look on my face, my cold hands squeezing imaginary boobs.

"Come here, my little Carmelita," I said.

"Don't call me that."

I pressed against her as she stood with her back toward the door. I don't know who we both were for a few seconds, but it felt raunchy and good. Elise playfully pushed me away and pressed the ice dispenser. Nothing came out.

"House is beginning to fall apart," she said. "Look at the white seams in the window. The insulation cracked."

We opened every cabinet and drawer, and though Elise would disagree with this fact, I will tell you that she committed the first act of violence.

She bent a spoon, twisted it into a *U* right in front of my face.

"Cheap," she said, as I snatched it out of her hand and tried to bend it back into the correct shape. That's the thing about cheap spoons: once you abuse them they stay abused.

"Come on, Elise," I said. "Show some respect."

I tossed the spoon back in its drawer and followed her out of the kitchen, past the dining room table. I pressed my palm onto the glass table, leaving a stubby green ghostprint of my fingers behind.

"Let's get out of here," she said. "It's creeping me out."

"I want to check out the downstairs bedroom. Come on. Then we'll go."

She followed me reluctantly, peering over my shoulder as I turned on the bedroom light, as if someone would be waiting for us there.

We walked around the queen-size bed the way people walk around art in museums. The thin, pastel-colored comforter was not pulled taut. The pillows and covers were rumpled in places, as if someone had been sitting there.

"That cactus looks like a prick," Elise said, kneeling down to touch one of its yellow spines. It only added another note of playful obscenity to the whole night.

"Motel art," I said, looking at the watercolor of the Indian squaw on her haggard horse.

Under the recessed lighting I could see the rain sparkling on Elise's black sweater, the cold drops suspended in the fibers. Suddenly she reached up and pulled the turtleneck off, tossing it on the green carpet. She unzipped her black jeans and mashed them down around her ankles, nearly tripping as she stepped out of them. I watched her sit on the bed and reach for the biggest pillow. She placed it under her stomach and playfully raised her ass in the air, her black panties reflecting two streaks of yellow light.

"Hurry up and fuck me," she said. "It's freezing in here."

I unbuttoned the jacket and tossed it on a chair in a corner of the room.

I pulled down her panties and ran my hand up the hollow of her back, feeling her arch as the heel of my hand traveled downward. I unzipped and pulled my cock and stroked it like some sordid john as I watched her look back at me. She was lightly playing with herself. I entered her as she hunched over some stranger's pillow. I dug my arms under the pillow and pulled her stomach toward me. For the first time in months, she reached back and grabbed my balls. I grabbed a handful of her hair and she didn't scream at me. We made up for three months of not having sex in less than ten minutes. I went down on her, her cold thighs pressed tight around my warm ears. I caught her looking in the mirror once, with a slight smile, pleased with the view, her hand pushing my forehead back.

"Do it nice," she said, playfully slapping my cheek, then she went back to looking at us in the mirror, her eyes closing. I got on top of her, my hands underneath, my mouth in her ear. I was already out of breath.

I finished outside of her, on the comforter. She kissed me and laughed. I distinctly remember that my chin was hooked over her bare shoulder and that my face was too close to hers to bring her eyes into focus. I slipped my hand into hers and she squeezed two of my fingers. We didn't lie there long because there was an odd, metallic odor and I remember telling Elise it was probably because the sheets hadn't been changed in a year. I poked my arms back into that stiff jacket and she pulled on the soaked sweater with a wince. We looked down at the wet spot on the blue sheet.

"We should probably take off the comforter," I said, looking at the mess I'd made on it.

"Why? No one lives here anymore."

I leaned over the bed and started to tug at an edge of the comforter when Elise reached for my arm and stopped me.

"We'll wash it and bring it back," I said. "Look at them. Don't they look like decent people?"

Elise had grown impatient with my attempts at playing housekeeper. She took a deep breath and stared at the photographs on the dresser. Mr. Swain and his fleshy face, the double fold of skin around the cheeks, a ready smile, white teeth. There was something about his eyes that seemed wrong. His wife was a narrow woman with a nest of silvery hair and a small mouth, wearing a diamond necklace, her hand oddly clenched on his shoulder, as if she were using him for support rather than showing affection.

"Let's just leave it," she said, walking toward the doorway and reaching for the switch to turn off the ceiling light. But I had already ripped the thin comforter off the bed. One more second and we would have been standing there in the dark. I would've just followed her out of the room, and none of this would've happened.

It was Elise who screamed before I noticed a thing. It was so obvious that I didn't see it at first. The dried bloodstains covered almost half of the sheet underneath. It wasn't until my eyes reached the blue of what was once a bedsheet that I realized what I was looking at.

Elise screamed again, then covered her mouth, looking at me with startled eyes. I followed her as she ran back toward the living room, but we never made it to the door. She doubled over and threw up.

"Don't panic. There's no one here," I told her, rubbing her back as she finished and looking up the winding staircase at the dark upstairs rooms.

I kept telling Elise to calm down, but as soon as she left the house, she started to run down the driveway. I caught her shoulder and she wheeled around.

"We have to go the other way," I said. "Down the deer path."

"I'm not walking that way. Someone's going to kill us."

I pointed at the dark outline of the house we had just left and tried to make her understand that no one was in there. We could call the police from Victor's place.

Elise continued walking down the driveway anyway, and I followed her. I couldn't see anything through the mist, just the trunks of the dark, wet elms that lined the driveway, the bark glistening with water. At the bottom, we pushed open a wooden gate that said SWAIN'S WAY and walked onto the shoulder of the highway. You could see the silent explosion of each car's brights long before they crested the hill and sped past us. We ducked our heads each time they passed, sure the drivers were watching us, probably making a mental note of the two of us, arm in arm on the road. We were both breathing heavily. That's the thing about getting the shit scared out of you. It's like you've run ten miles.

I think it was about 11:30 when we got back to the house. Elise took a hot shower. I raked through Victor's liquor cabinet for the last of his booze. I poured some Bacardi into a glass and drank it warm and straight as I looked out the window in the living room. The lights in the upstairs room of that house, the ones on the timer, had long since turned themselves off, but I quickly figured out why there still seemed to be a dim yellow reflection floating through the trees.

"Left the light on in the bedroom," I said to myself, picking up the binoculars I had placed on the coffee table. I scanned the whole house again through the mist, momentarily startled by a dark shape in another upstairs window. I stayed on it until I realized that it was probably a mirror. At the very least, it was reassuringly rectangular, and not human-shaped.

I knew, of course, that I'd have to go back. It wasn't just the light. My wife had thrown up on the floor. We'd left a comforter balled up in a stranger's bedroom. A bloody mattress exposed as if we'd known just what we were looking for.

Upstairs, I heard the sound of my wife showering, the splatter of water as she shifted positions, the sound of the water stopping. It sounded as if she were coughing for a moment. It took me a few seconds to realize what it was.

I walked upstairs, knocked on the bathroom door. Slowly pushed it open.

She was sitting there on the toilet in a white bathrobe, eyes red-rimmed with tears. She looked at me warily, as if I had somehow caused the whole situation.

"If this gets ugly," she said, "I'm never going to forgive you."

I let a night pass. Twelve hours in which I tried not to think of the situation in the house next door.

I was boiling Campbell's tomato soup in a small saucepan when I heard Elise's agitated voice on the answering machine, calling from the hospital.

"If you don't call them," she said. "I will."

I shut the burner off. I wasn't interested in the pale orange soup anymore. Its bubbling circumference.

I picked up the phone and imagined myself dialing 911. I think this should be taken into consideration, just how close I came to doing the right thing.

I put the phone back down because I needed to rehearse what I would say. For instance, how could I explain the semen on the sheets we had left in the room, or the fact that my wife had thrown up on the floor, or the wine bottle somewhere out there in the woods, or the fact that I had used a stranger's house as a marital aid? Conceivably, if I called 911, I might be in prison by the end of the night, and for all I knew, the bloodstain on the bed had an explanation. Maybe a disturbed relative had cut his wrist in that guest room, or maybe a beloved son had blown his brains out, sending his family into exodus. Then I would be the craven next-door neighbor who had decided to break in and have sex on his deathbed.

If this had happened on the road somewhere, if we had

gone exploring near a vacation rental, it would have been different. But with Victor ill, we couldn't just drive away from the house next door.

What ended up happening that afternoon was that I walked right into another blind spot. Instead of calling the police, I poured myself a second Bacardi and Coke and watched some famous chef make Beef Carbonnade on television. I found a pair of yellow kitchen gloves and pulled them on. Then I laced up my sneakers, stuck one of Victor's king-sized linens under my jacket, and left the house with a dollar-store mop and a soapy bucket of water. It was almost dark when I climbed over the fence and found the deer path.

I waited inside the front door of the house for a long time, just listening. I could feel my heart pulsing in my neck and wrist as I tried to distinguish outside and inside noise, the sound of the sloshing waves from the sound of the refrigerator in the kitchen suddenly kicking in. But I was still jumpy and nervous, crying out "Hello" when I thought I heard something upstairs. I convinced myself it was a pine tree branch scraping against the window.

The mess on the living room floor was relatively easy to take care of. I flipped on the chandelier in the double-height room and mopped up the crusty trail on the floor. There wasn't even that much to clean up.

I left the bucket and mop by the door, admired the shiny rectangle of cleanliness I had created on the white floor, and walked to the bedroom. The ceiling light was still on there, glowering over the stain on the bedsheet. There was no question it was blood. It flaked slightly in the quilted ridges, and I got the impression that it had penetrated deep into the mattress.

I was right. When I peeled back the sheet, the mattress underneath was saturated with blood. The relatively faint light cast by the recessed light made it look more black than red. The bloodstain stretched across the mattress in chromatic layers of varying darkness, even turning the small white buttons red. I leaned forward and caught that metallic odor again, the tang of it sticking inside my nostrils.

Pulling Victor's queen-size sheet over one corner of the bed, and then another, I stretched it over the stain. I leaned over the bed again, stretching toward the third corner, and lost my balance slightly. My face was inches away from the bloodiest part of the mattress, and I flinched at its metallic smell, like old silverware left in a drawer for years. It wasn't as overpowering as a pint of moldy sour cream, but it was still distinct. Snapping the last corner of the bedsheet underneath, I stepped back, expecting to see a fist-sized circle of wet red blood mar the clean sheet, then other fists appearing all over the cotton. But it stayed dry as long as I looked at it.

I balled up the bloody sheet and stuck it under my jacket. I put the comforter back on the bed and even stretched it over the two pillows. I zipped up my jacket and then I did one last tour of the house, because I told myself I'd never see it again. I suppose if I wasn't wearing those yellow gloves I would've just left. Instead I opened the dresser drawers in the bedroom, found nothing of interest except for a flowery dress and an eggshell-blue cashmere sweater, and closed them again.

You won't have any particular interest in the many objects I picked up and put down in that house that late afternoon. A half-empty bottle of conditioner. A frilly box of soap.

I walked into the kitchen, retrieving Elise's bent spoon, stuffed it in my pocket. I slowly walked up the winding staircase, admiring the glassy guts of the chandelier. At the top of the stairs I flipped on another bank of lights. There were two more bedrooms, a sitting room, a study. As I opened and closed the dresser drawers in the two bedrooms, knelt down and inspected the spaces under the beds, it began to occur to me that the only exceptional quality of the house was the bloodstain.

It was the kind of place that had a candelabra on the side of the bathtub. One too many Ken Follett novels in the sitting room. A wicker basket of light jazz CDs. There was a collection of creased Fodor's travel books. Venice. Provence. The Grand Canyon. There were DVDs on a shelf near the flat-panel television that were equally unremarkable and fairly ancient. *Rain Man, Black Hawk Down, Fried Green Tomatoes, Shine.* I opened them, just in case some porn had been hidden in one, but every one was in its right place.

It was impossible to reconcile the situation in the downstairs bedroom with everything else I saw in the house. There was a photograph on a marble table in the sitting room. His wife was standing on his left, leaning against him slightly, her narrow face pinched into a smile, a silk scarf covering her head. Her right hand was crumpled around the handle of an aluminum cane.

I opened another dresser drawer, peeling back the paper lining it. I heard one of the closet doors knock slightly against its runner and I straightened instantly. I had to force myself to move toward it, as if I were encased, suddenly, in some kind of mental ice. When I slid it back, there was nothing inside except a thickly bunched row of padded jackets and a black dress covered with red roses. Everywhere I looked in that house, there was some version of a fake flower. Flowers on the plates on the wall. Painted flowers on the floor. Flowers on dresses. I had the feeling the wife was covering herself in them after some tragic event, or could see some terrible event coming. But that was just guesswork.

Flipping off the lights, I grabbed the bucket and mop and walked outside.

Near the deer path, I chucked the dirty water into a bed of dead pine needles and made my way back to Victor's house. It had begun to snow. Large wet flakes falling on the dry branches around me without a sound. Out on the bay, there were hardly any waves. A black rash of seaweed visible just underneath the water, and a few ducks slowly moving toward one another. I wondered if it was out of affection, or because of the current.

It doesn't cost me anything to admit it now. Elise always looked very pretty when she was sad. I think it depends on what type of face you have. I don't look too bad when I'm feeling down myself, but Elise's brown eyes seemed to grow browner, her eyelashes longer. Don't believe all that garbage you hear about happy couples. The sad ones know more, feel everything twice as much. That's why they hardly speak. They can share pain just by twitching their mouths a certain way, or choose not to reassure each other with a single word that used to provide comfort. When it comes right down to it, misery is just another art form, as hard to perfect as any other craft, only we aim to leave nothing behind. We're the copper thieves of our own houses, ripping out our own wires. Slowly, we've stolen the best parts of each other, carted ourselves away.

Part of me was admiring how uncertain and almost girlish she looked as she sat there in her coat in the kitchen chair, snowflakes vanishing on her shoulders as she watched me stand there with my mop. Part of me was hearing myself explain my grand theories.

"I have no idea," I said. "But I think he blew his wife away with the shotgun in the closet."

"Why didn't you call the police?"

"And what I'm thinking is that she had cancer or something, because she had a scarf on her head. So maybe he gets tired of her being a burden and being ill and he just puts her out of her misery."

"Answer me."

"Because it's breaking and entering."

"We just walked in. We didn't break anything."

"It's still a crime. They'd laugh at us and throw us in jail."

Elise looked down at the bare table in front of her, shook her head slightly.

"It's something worse now," she said. "It's like we're helping cover something up."

I asked her how her father was, something that would make her feel like she wasn't a criminal.

"Worse," she said.

"Matter-of-days kind of thing?" I said, realizing instantly that it was the wrong way to put it.

"He's my father. He's not a thing."

We argued after that. Then we argued about arguing. I wondered if the only place we really had a chance was in that house that wasn't ours. In a bedroom we could never sleep in.

"My clients are leaving me," she said, narrowing her eyes as if she could see them, changing their minds after all the work she had done with their children.

"They'll come back."

"No, they won't," she said, finally pushing away the chair and standing up. "They never do."

There was a big fir tree at the end of that cul-de-sac on Ocean View Road. It had been wrapped with strings of big colored lights. There was an older couple who lived on that property, but we'd never met them. Maybe we'd seen their car pass by once or twice. That week before Christmas, Elise and I were coming back from the supermarket in Hampton Bays and saying nothing as we turned right on the dark road that led to Victor's house. We drove past all the darkened summer homes, dim blue lights lining one massive driveway, as if it were a curved runway. Their rich owners, I assumed, were shoulder to shoulder in the city, in paneled rooms that teemed with holiday conversation, with candlelight doubled in mirrors and caterers carrying silver trays. This was the winter season they would never see, a chilly hollowness that their caretakers could hardly be bothered with, letting bagged newspapers build up against white gates.

As I drove toward Victor's house, I thought to myself that I could have picked any of these dark homes. Instead I'd had sex in a murder scene, in one of the less impressive houses. I was an idiot.

I was driving, my jaw set, thinking of that porcelain pig and its snouty grin, the promise that the best was yet to come. When we took the last right, we could see it through all the dead branches. That amazing tree. I pulled the car over and we just stared at it in silence. There was no need to say anything. It made us that happy, and when an unhappy couple is happy, it's almost like having a vision, or speaking in tongues. It's like you've somehow burst to the surface on someone's shoulders and been given a few moments to see everything you've been missing.

I felt like I should write a note and leave it on their driveway, thanking them for taking the time to wrap that enormous, perfect tree in so many goddamn perfect lights.

When we got to our own driveway, heard the cold splash of gravel against the tires, Elise started to cry. It all came out then, the whole tangle of everything she'd kept bottled up. The way her father had touched her when she was young. How much more she wanted to be in life than a speech therapist.

How she probably couldn't even do that now. For a moment, I didn't think it would come around to me, but it sure did. I couldn't make a living. I couldn't understand her. I had cost her the baby by making her wait until she was too old. And now it had been my moronic idea to go into that house. We'd probably end up broke and in jail. Then she confessed one more thing that stuck with me for days. An ex-boyfriend from college had found her on Facebook and they'd been e-mailing. It wasn't serious yet, but she found herself thinking of him more than me lately.

"Who?" I shouted.

"Curt," she said.

"Kurt Weidenfeld?"

"Curt Page."

"You're fucking kidding me," I said, wishing her face would suddenly twist into a smile and we'd still have one last chance to be a couple again. But she wasn't lying. Even Kurt Weidenfeld wouldn't have been as bad. Curt Page was a pompous, beady-eyed prick with an overgrown mullet and an earring who we'd briefly shared a loft with in South Williamsburg. He was a copy editor for some long-extinct tech magazine, and he was constantly pestering people to read his unfinished novel. He had opinions with a capital O and exhaled deeply after each statement he'd make, as if his words were so decked out with brilliance that they might stall before they reached the listener unless he gave them that long, extra puff of air.

One of his opinions was that everyone should be allowed to carry a concealed weapon. There was a .357 he proudly showed us, that he kept under his bed, and an old, lovingly polished Smith & Wesson that had once belonged to his late father. Once our other roommates found that out, we had a house meeting and he was kicked out. It did cross my mind that Curt might blow us all away before he hit the highway, but in the morning, the only ominous thing he left was a handwritten note for Elise, profoundly thanking her for encouraging him to continue with his novel. He promised to keep in touch and then, in his uniquely condescending way, told her that she'd realize, sooner or later, that they were meant for each other. Even though he'd split, I could hear the long exhale after that one.

"He's on the road again," Elise said, as if this zero was channeling Jack Kerouac.

"Curt Page is on the road. Does the media know about this?"

Elise laughed at that, and for a moment I thought she'd give in, the way all couples do when they still love each other.

"He's going through a painful divorce," she said. There was too much sympathy in her voice. I thought that asking for any more information about Curt would be like waving the white flag in some way. Admitting that he'd become the most minor issue in our troubled marriage.

"I didn't know he'd even gotten married."

I climbed out of the car and slammed the door. I think we would have gotten into an argument that would have finally finished us off for good, but it never happened. It never happened because I noticed something troubling directly in front of me. Through the scrub pine I could see the light in the window of our neighbor's house, and then, about fifty feet away, the headlights of a parked pickup truck, streaming in a thicket of nearby branches, its exhaust whipped away by a gust of cold wind, then coiling again.

Looking back, I think we did the wrong thing. As soon as we were safe inside Victor's house, we turned off every light. We ran around whispering commands to each other and nearly tripping over the ends of rugs. Then we stood by the sides of the living room window, and I mashed the binoculars against my eyes.

"What do you see?" Elise said. "What are they doing?"

I twisted the center focus knob on the binoculars, heard the tap of the lens against my own glasses. A blurry ghost of a lighted window became a sharp rectangle, but I just missed focusing on the figure that left the room.

"There was somebody up there," Elise said. "Some guy."

She was doing better with her naked eyes. I twisted the focus knob again. The house was ablaze now. Someone was flicking switches in every room, and this time I caught a bit of him as he moved past the window of one of the guest rooms. He was thickly built, Hispanic, and his mouth was moving as he turned and glanced over his shoulder, as if he were giving someone else commands. Another face, also Hispanic, appeared in the room, the rest of his body cut off by the window frame.

"Let me see," Elise said.

I handed her the binoculars and watched her watching them.

"They're back downstairs," she said. I reached out for the binoculars and tugged them away. I raised them to my eyes just in time to see their backs as they walked through the living room. I panned the binoculars to the truck idling outside, an F-150 with oversized wheels, the dark color impossible to discern. There were two white letters on the side, joined I thought by a fancy ampersand, but at that angle I couldn't make it out. I was still focused on it when the larger of the two men walked right into my field of vision.

"They're leaving," Elise whispered. "Both of them."

But they didn't leave. They sat in the truck, smoke from

the exhaust pipe curling into the air. I couldn't see through the rear windows.

"What's going on?" Elise said.

"They're just sitting there. There's some company name written on the truck, but I can't make it out in the dark."

I have no way of knowing exactly how much time passed, but it must have been ten minutes at least. Then the driver's door opened again. He climbed out and walked to the house, and I followed him with the binoculars. Alone this time, he made his way through the same rooms. Once, I saw his shoulder jerk and his mouth pull back into a grimace, as if he had just kicked something. One by one, he turned off the lights. In the bedrooms, in the sitting room, in the guest room, even the light that had been on the timer.

"He's leaving again," I said to Elise, watching him angrily pull open the truck's door and climb back in.

A moment later, the triangle of brake lights flared and the truck reversed, pulled away, carrying its own saucer of light all the way back down the long driveway.

We lay in the dark, on her father's bed, arguing about what we had seen. But it wasn't the normal kind of argument we always had. It was filled with excitement, and every time we disagreed about something, it was only so we could revise and perfect the little we had seen, the little we had to go on.

"I think the heavier one was wearing a Carhartt jacket. Tan," I said.

"It wasn't tan," she said. "It was darker than that, and he was wearing a sweatshirt under it. Baggy jeans."

"About one hundred eighty pounds."

"Heavier than that."

"A baseball cap, right?"

"Yes," she said. "Blue, with some kind of white letter."

We were holding hands, her fingers squeezing mine, then letting go, each time something else occurred to her. We both agreed that we had never gotten a good look at the other guy.

"What do you think?" I said.

"They're working for somebody."

"You know what I think?" I said, my big theory seizing up my throat like a little kid.

"What?"

"Maybe it's Swain. Maybe they've got him tied up somewhere and he's gotten something valuable hidden there somewhere."

"I don't want to even picture that," Elise said. "Maybe it's something smaller. Maybe they're just ordinary thieves."

"But they didn't leave with anything. They just drove off."

Elise pulled her fingers away from mine and reached toward the lamp on the bedside table.

"Leave the binoculars alone tonight," she said. "And promise you'll stay right beside me."

I promised her that I would, but an hour later, I swung my legs to the floor and walked as quietly as I could to the window. The light in the upstairs bedroom of Swain's home was on. I picked up the binoculars and glanced over at Elise's dark shape, curled up in the bed. Either she was breathing steadily in her sleep or staring at me. I couldn't tell. But when I turned the focus knob and pulled the white wall of the bedroom into focus, her breath hitched.

"Hey," she said, and for a moment I thought she was talking to me. I was about to apologize when I realized she was talking to someone in her sleep, warning them in a stream of mumbled words I couldn't make out.

On Christmas Eve, I stood in Swain's upstairs bedroom, staring at the file cabinet that the intruder had kicked over. The light was already fading in the empty house, shadows unrolling themselves from the walls. I didn't dare touch a switch. I got on my knees and sifted through the paperwork strewn all over the room. The men had clearly been looking for something more valuable than a bunch of old bank statements, none of which contained a whole account number that would have been useful to them. They were all from the joint account of a Richard and Martha Swain, the balance of which was $143,000 in 2010. There were statements from 2009 and 2008, and those balances were noticeably larger, averaging more than $900,000. I carefully folded the most recent and stuffed it in my pocket and left the rest lying on the off-white carpet, four divots pressed into it, a memory of where the cabinet, unkicked, had once stood.

They'd opened all the drawers of the dresser, and even out of frustration thrown one onto the master bed. The drawers in the other room were pulled open as well. A closet in the upstairs hallway was opened and an armful of clothes tossed on the floor. They couldn't have been anything more than amateur thieves. Maybe they'd been tempted to drive slowly up Swain's driveway when they saw what a wreck the entrance was, with its strewn tree limbs and crumbling entry gate.

Walking over to the window, I waved down at Elise, who was standing a few feet away from the flagstone steps that led to the front door, her arms folded against her chest. Seeing the men search the house the night before, we had become convinced there was something valuable there we had missed.

I gave her a thumbs-up, just to show her I was okay. I headed back down the staircase, with the folder under my arm. Far out on the bay, a seam of cold sunlight had broken across the water. I was standing on one of the bottom steps, transfixed by the tenderness of the light that momentarily filled this house that would never be mine. A faint yellow light glowed from within the crystal chandelier, as if someone had turned up the dimmer switch.

I've always believed that the worst things happen when you are most off guard. I felt the warmth of the light on my face as I walked across the living room one more time and pressed my forehead against the cold glass of the sliding door, the same cold pane I had peered in just weeks before. It's funny, but I saw my own face looking in, my own face looking out. Nothing had changed, really, except that I had dragged my wife into an uncomfortable situation.

I remember thinking that my willingness to cross certain boundaries had probably saved my marriage. For months, we'd watched television and cooked frozen dinners while waiting for her father to die, and when we bothered to talk it was as if we were acquaintances passing each other on some windswept street. What were we going to say? Nothing of the smallest significance was happening out there, except the occasional sounds of clam shells being dropped on Victor's all-weather deck by hungry seagulls.

And now it had fallen into our laps: Swain's house, which I now thought of as a double exposure. Both homes now superimposed on the same plate.

I was still standing by the sliding glass door, and I remember watching a fishing boat cross the bay, the noise of its motor vibrating the glass door slightly. I also remember turning and seeing Elise through the window of the front door, Elise perfectly framed there, shrugging in frustration at me, because I was probably taking too long. I held up my index finger to let her know I'd be done in a minute.

I walked into the kitchen, past the breakfast nook, where the placemats were still laid out, looking for anything that the two men might have left behind. The only sign they had left of their search was a single kitchen drawer left open. For some reason, I closed it.

The pig still held its chalkboard sign and its promise. I tried the door that led to the basement, but it was locked.

I walked back the way I had come, and then I saw him, standing just outside the sliding glass door, watching me with a kind of pleased amazement as I turned toward him.

When you aren't supposed to be somewhere and you see someone you shouldn't see, the best idea is probably to get out of there as fast as humanly possible. But I froze. I just stood there and looked at him. He pulled down the bill of his blue baseball cap and smiled at me, almost flirtatiously. Then he knocked on the glass, not particularly aggressively, and indicated the lock on the handle that I would have no problem flicking open. The most violent men have no idea that they're terrible actors. No great voice ever boomed out of the sky and told them, I suppose, that they couldn't be both things.

His face, darkened by shadows, was turned sideways now, and he was saying something that was muted by the glass. I could see the moisture of his breath expand on the window. He tapped the glass with his knuckles again, a little harder, as if I were a little thick and didn't get the point. When I took a step back, he shook his head, and then he kicked it all in.

Really, in the end, it's all about a lack of patience. Patience with each other. Patience with the world. Patience with ourselves.

I was running when I heard the glass break. It must have taken him three kicks to clear a path through what was once an intact sliding door. I remember that there seemed to be an exact pause between each kick, as if he had done this professionally somewhere before. By that time I was out of the house, screaming my wife's name. But she was nowhere in sight. I should have waited, even if I could hear his boots crackling on the pieces of glass inside.

"Elise," I kept yelling.

But I was running.

After escaping, I got lost in the woods above the bay. I waited until it got dark and then I found my way to the highway. I walked along the shoulder, not particularly caring if a van pulled ahead of me and braked hard and I was dragged away. I should have called the police the moment I got back to Victor's house, but I guess I wasn't thinking straight. If I was thinking straight, I wouldn't have sat there in the dark, weeping and talking to myself and drinking bourbon. If I was thinking straight, why would I have climbed over the fence again and walked down the deer path? Why would I have walked around the half-empty pool and right up to the broken sliding door? I walked right back in the way I had come and the moon blazed brighter than the winter sun, showing me the outline of each piece of glass. I picked up a piece just to prove to myself what had really happened hours earlier. The front door was still open, and I walked out and hollered her name again and again. Drunk now, I was as brave as I'd been cowardly before.

I walked back into the house and I remember the first thing I did was turn on the chandelier. The only time I would ever do so. The whole house seemed to glitteringly await my next move. Shards of light hanging on the walls.

I picked up an iron poker from the side of the fireplace. I waved it through the air once, taking a practice swing, then a faster one, until I could hear the rush of stale air against it.

My third swing caught the Cleopatra statue flush, almost decapitating her smug wooden head. My fourth swing was an overhand smash, right into Swain's dining room table. I watched white cracks spider outward. I lifted the poker over my head again and this time the table shattered, shards of it flying into my hair. It sounds crazy, but I felt like I was getting somewhere. I aimed the harpoon tip of the poker into each flowery plate on the wall, closing my eyes as each one exploded. I was sweating now. I was in a rhythm.

In the kitchen, I faced that shiny porcelain pig, with its snouty smile and chef's hat and its THE BEST IS YET TO COME chalkboard. I touched its crinkled nose once and then I reached back to obliterate it, but I didn't. I let it just sit there, gleaming.

In one of the kitchen drawers I found a large box of safety matches. It's an oxymoron that delights me now, like friendly fire, hard water, and easy death.

I had this idea you just strike one and a house burns down, but I struck ten, twenty, thirty, holding them against the corner of the counter, underneath chairs, against fucking curtains. Finally, I collapsed on the kitchen floor. I couldn't even set a fringed cushion on fire.

I remember that my fingers were raw and singed as I walked back around the pool and found the deer path. It wasn't until I'd climbed over Victor's fence that I noticed something flash behind me. A curtain, I realized, in the kitchen window, in flames. I watched it in thrilled amazement, I have to admit. And then it extinguished itself.

Convinced the darkness next door wouldn't be disturbed again, I lay down on the sofa in Victor's living room. I dreamed two things that night: that the house finally burned down with a sound like an endlessly breaking wave, and that my wife was safe and had returned home, gently squeezing my shoulder as I slept. Even in my dreams, I knew only one could be true.

"You ran away," Elise said.

We were both sitting on the couch. It was so late it was early, the sky tugging itself away from the blackness of the bay and scrub pine. Three dark scraps that may have been seagulls or dead leaves floated upward and disappeared.

Elise's wool sweater was lanced with pine needles and ripped near the shoulder. Her sneakers and blue jeans were soaking wet, up to her knees, as if she had made her way out of the sea.

She was impossible to hold or kiss. She tilted away from me, completely detached from how thankful I was.

"I was looking for you," I said. "I went back."

"I was hiding in the woods," she said, "when you ran past."

We'd already been over it. There was no point in comparing our cowardice. She said that as soon as she saw him, she went around the house as I walked into the kitchen. In fact, if I had looked, instead of closing some stupid drawer, I would have seen her fifteen feet away, outside, waving her arms.

"But when he kicked in the door," I said. "You ran."

"*You* ran. You ran right by me, yelling my name, as if that would do any fucking good."

I had felt bad enough afterward, remembering how I'd shouted for her as I saved my own skin in the woods. It was terrible to imagine her as a front-row spectator, cowering there as I vanished.

"I went back," I said, looking through the window, the outlines of the chimneys of the house next door visible, its three peaks, unburnt. A bit of blue winking at me in one of its windows.

"You went back," she said derisively. "After it was safe, after they were gone, after I could've been killed."

"We both could have been killed. We could still be killed. They could be watching us right now."

It was the only thing that stopped the argument. It was the only technique that seemed to save us in those last days. The threat of something worse happening.

"Maybe you should run now," she said, plucking a pine needle out of her ruined sweater. "Get it over with."

The light from the table lamp was fading in our laps as the sky dialed itself a shade lighter. When I remember our last days, I always try to imagine what would've happened if, just once, we were who we were supposed to be. In bed. Sleeping. Like a normal married couple. But I don't think we would have been as dependent on each other as we were at that moment. We still had a secret that no one else knew, and it was getting bigger every day.

"I tried to burn the house down," I said, touching the dry mud on her knee.

"That's nice, sweetie," she said sarcastically, tracing my fingers with hers, her voice hoarse from the exhaustion of waiting in the woods for hours. She stood up and I followed her, just as the flaring sun rose above the inlet, and we climbed the stairs and went to bed.

There was one more thing she said that morning, right before she fell asleep in her sweater, her socks crowned with dirt.

"There was a deer," she said softly. "It must have stood there for an hour. Just watching *me.*"

It wasn't till after she had fallen asleep that I realized it was Christmas.

We slept fitfully the entire night, sure that the man was near us, ready to attack again. It was only near morning, when the faintest sunlight had begun to appear behind the blinking radio beacon on the inlet, that I really fell asleep.

It might have been an hour or two later when I woke again and saw that Elise was sitting up in bed.

"Maybe we just cut and run," she said. "Leave this house. Let my father die alone."

"I don't see you doing that."

The truth was, I didn't see *myself* doing it. I was all in now. If we escaped to Brooklyn, it would be even worse. She'd leave me next. I felt like I had to give a very convincing pep talk that would persuade her to stay put.

"You don't know me."

It was a line that she had used before. It's what a couple on the brink always say to each other, as if to protect themselves from judgment after knowing each other for so many years. *Yeah, sure, I don't know you.*

"You have a really fucked-up family," I said, massaging her neck with the back of my thumb. She reached behind her shoulder and lightly grabbed my wrist, squeezing it twice. This would have been the time to tell her stories of how screwed-up my own family was, but compared to hers, they were about as sinister as pancakes on Sunday.

"I know," she said. "Sometimes I feel like they kidnapped me when I was a kid. Took me from some beach or something when my real family was playing in the waves."

That was all she wanted to say. Her eyes slowly closed and she fell asleep, her body jerking once before she started to dream again. I wondered if she was dreaming of the beach, or a fairground, or a schoolyard, or any of the other places children feel most safe.

I stood up and walked to the window, picking up the binoculars and searching every corner of the property, and then what I could see in the scrub of the gully that led to the house next door. But no one was lurking anywhere.

On my way toward the bathroom, I noticed the family photograph I had never paid much attention to, sitting on the dresser. It was a fading snapshot of Victor, Elise, and Ryder, her younger brother. The kids might have been fourteen and twelve, I guessed. Her brother's eyes are almost closed, his mouth parted as if he is speaking to the photographer. His arm is thrown around his taller sister's shoulder. The display of affection sticks out only because Victor stands at least a foot away from them, with an uncertain smile on his face, as if he had just happened to wander into the shot, like some sort of tourist instead of a father.

That day, we both managed to get through a visit with her father, watching him open two presents. As drugged as he was, it had taken him forever. Elise had given him a cashmere sweater. I'd given him a wallet and a silvery-wrapped bottle of Freixenet. He put them back into the wrong boxes and weeded the cheerful reindeer wrapping paper from his bedspread. Out in the hallway, a strand of lights was winking on and off and an orderly was whistling the first bars of "Winter Wonderland" again and again.

"Well, that'll do it," he finally said. "Very thoughtful of you."

For a moment, just for a moment, I had felt sorry for him. Maybe it was the way his pale cheek doubled against itself as he flicked away the last offensive bits of wrapping paper, or the way he raised his chin back up, almost like an expectant boy, as his daughter leaned over to kiss his forehead. She patted his limp hand and told me it was time to go.

"I left a dollar in it," I said, pointing to the box he'd put the wallet I'd given him in. "For good luck. Don't be offended."

He didn't say anything nasty this time. He didn't have to. He just pursed his lips slightly, to let me know he was trying very hard to hold his tongue. *Of all the people,* I knew he was thinking, *to give me luck.*

Before I left the room, though, he called my name. I turned and saw that he was gripping the bottle of cheap champagne.

"Take this with you," he said. "I don't drink anymore. I'm surprised Elise didn't tell you that."

"I've got a lot on my mind, Daddy," she said, leaning over to give him a quick kiss on his waxy forehead. She took the offending bottle out of his hand and we ended up leaving it near a potted plant in the hallway.

We drove home in silence, and I slowed as I passed the fir with the Christmas lights.

"Do you think they have children?" Elise said as she looked at it.

"I don't know," I said, annoyed at the question. "Why would it matter?"

"It's a little self-indulgent if they're just doing it for themselves."

I let the argument go. It was Christmas, after all. I didn't want to spend it having a conversation about the importance of children. That's why we hadn't bothered with a tree ourselves. I knew Elise would imagine the little one-year-old boy who would never get to see it. It was just over a year before, with Elise pregnant, that we'd come up with a final list of names: Rusty. Derek. Jack. Frank. It was possibly the happiest week of our lives. We'd sit in the small living room of our apartment on Bergen Street, oblivious to the nasty argument breaking out in the apartment next door. Elise, I remember distinctly, had a small pad of paper in her hand and a smile she couldn't keep off her face the whole night. We debated each name as if we were debating a real person, because a Frank was very different from a Derek, and a Jack would surely be a boy who would be admired but not necessarily need as much company as a Rusty.

We got it down to two, Jack and Frank, and then we promised we'd make the final selection the following day. Elise went to work as usual. Early in the afternoon, just as I was leading a particularly polite and attractive Asian couple to my wedding tree, I got a call from her on my cell phone. She was having terrible cramps. The doctor had told her to come in.

Some emergencies take only a second to develop—a car crash, for instance. You get the picture instantly; you might even be able to shout something or brace yourself. But I've always thought the worst emergencies are the ones that start almost innocently, as if the day were two joined plates of ice that had just begun to separate. The worst emergencies have always made me feel like I'm still in control at first.

I was slightly alarmed after Elise's phone call, and I knew I would take the subway to Manhattan and meet her at Saint Vincent's, but I still felt that the day had nothing vicious in store for me. I wouldn't have lifted the Nikon to my eye and urged the Asian couple to move closer together. They called a few days later, to ask me about the photographs, and I told them what had happened. Elise had slept for two drugged days after the miscarriage, but I had wandered around the hallways of the hospital, exhausted but filled with the need to speak to someone, anyone, about our personal tragedy. I was under the mistaken impression that the story itself might be revised, and that by starting at the beginning again I might arrive at a different ending.

"Do you remember when my cell phone rang?" I asked the husband I had photographed. "She was calling me from her office. She told me not to panic. She was just having some cramps."

He kept saying "sorry" as he listened, and I think he realized he couldn't ask me when he might see the photographs. He wanted to get off the phone; I could hear it in the murmur of his voice. It made me angry.

"What if I wasn't standing by that fucking tree?" I said. "What if I'm sitting at home and when she calls I drive her to the city. It saves time. Wouldn't that have saved time?"

"I don't think you can blame yourself," the man said softly. He wanted to hang up now. Maybe when I got over my grief I'd get around to mailing him a refund.

"See, this is the thing," I said. "I do blame myself. I blame you too. I blame your wife. Why the fuck did you call me that day? What the fuck do you people find so fascinating about Prospect Park? Why can't you get your photographs taken outside a church or something, like normal people? If you didn't have this stupid obsession about my park I'd be holding my son right now."

He was a patient, sympathetic man. He must have listened to me rage for fifteen solid minutes as I paced in the small glassed-in alcove of the hospital, turning away from the elevators each time they opened, because I couldn't look at one more joyful relative without wanting to strangle them. At the very end of the conversation, when I had run out of ways to tear apart a man I didn't even know, I sat on a small wood bench by the window, pinched the bridge of my nose, and went to pieces.

"I'm still here," he said softly. "Okay? I'm still here."

I was touched by that, I really was.

But I have to tell you, my wedding-photographer gig started to go south after that. There was even another photographer, a black guy I vaguely knew, who'd taken over my tree. I watched him taking pictures there one day, trying to use humor to loosen the smile of a bride who kept lifting her frothy white dress off the carpet of yellow leaves, casting nervous glances at the wet black bark of that tree.

"I need you to look at me," the photographer said. "Forget about the tree. It's not going to hurt you."

I'll tell you one more thing: we named our little boy Frank. We called him that when they gave us a few minutes alone with him at the end, his eyes shut, his face blue, one small fist touching his chin.

I built a fire on Christmas night and Elise made dinner. Every now and then I could hear Elise lift the aluminum foil covering the turkey, and the hiss as the liquid fell around it. I was crouched by the snapping logs, thinking of the dollar I'd left in Victor's wallet and the fact that he'd probably thrown it all in the wastebasket as soon as I left the room.

We were speaking to each other while we concentrated on our mundane tasks. Voices raised over simmering turkey and the snapping fire so that we could hear each other from the different rooms. We'd already exchanged Christmas presents. A belt I didn't need. A half-price coat that she pretended to admire in the mirror before finally telling me the sleeves were too long. You can tell a lot about a marriage by the gifts couples give each other. I was always reminded of how little she knew about what I wanted, what little I knew of what she really desired.

"I've got the store credit receipt in my wallet," I said, watching her sadly fold up the sleeves of the coat. She looked expensively homeless.

Store credit receipt, I thought to myself. Three words that would really cut the distance that was stretching between us. But yet there was a receipt in my wallet, and I had bought her a coat on sale at the Bloomingdale's in Hampton Bays. And in some parallel universe they hang husbands for that. Briefly, I felt awful. But then my gift had been a thin leather belt that she finally confessed she had found at half price in the ladies' section.

"You bought me a woman's belt?" I said, threading it through the loops in my jeans and fastening the shiny rectangular buckle.

"It's plated," she said, a little defensively, still hovering near me in that overlarge coat with its green dangling price tag. "I've got the receipt for that too."

"It's perfect," I said, facing the large mirror in the entrance hall and pulling up my shirt so that I could see the silver buckle, winking at me in the lamplight. "I want to be buried wearing it, actually."

"I'll try to remember that," she said.

I gave her a quick thank-you kiss on the cheek.

"I should check on the turkey," she said.

At around eight in the evening on Christmas Day, I sat deep in Victor's overstuffed sofa, staring at yet another bottle of ancient liquor I had rescued from his cabinet. It was a bottle of Cutty Sark I held in my hands, and every so often I'd set it down on the floor and try to twist off the cap of the wretched half-empty bottle.

"You don't need two signatures to empty a joint account," I said. I twisted with all my might again and the cap finally came loose from the neck of the green bottle. I grabbed the glass on the side table and filled it halfway, trying not to notice three brown particles that floated to the top.

Elise and I had been talking about the bank papers we'd found next door, and whether Mr. or Mrs. Swain could have emptied the mutual account.

"How do you know?"

I couldn't tell her exactly how I knew, because it would

have ruined our dinner. After the miscarriage, we'd had a fight about money that had grown so serious I spent a week at a friend's house in Manhattan, researching divorce in New York State and getting to know terms like *wasteful disbursement of assets*.

"First of all," I said. "Let's just say he empties the account."

The Cutty Sark wasn't awful. I fished one of the dusty particles off my tongue and flicked it onto the rug.

"Or she empties it," Elise said.

"Maybe she blew *him* away."

Elise shrugged and popped back into the kitchen, and I continued to pore over the bank statement. For all I knew, he'd blown himself away after some financial turmoil. Maybe he was a real-estate tycoon in Atlanta and this was his second home. Maybe the property next door had been foreclosed on. The only thing I felt I knew for sure at that point was that the house hadn't been lived in for a couple of years. I could tell by the layer of dust on the counters, the shrunken onion, the backdated bank statements. If I'd succeeded in burning it down, I would have probably done everyone a favor.

"Something awful happened there," I said. "It's not like there were just a few drops of blood."

Elise didn't say anything. I knew she didn't like being reminded of the blood. The careful way someone had stretched a clean blanket over the caked fluid, as if it were a temporary fix and they were coming back. But by making a decision not to call the police immediately, we had implicated ourselves. It was as simple as that.

"It has something to do with the Swains," I heard Elise finally say. "That's all I know."

I pictured Richard Swain leaning over a new mistress in the fighting chair of a fishing boat, bobbing on the limpid waters off the Florida Keys, helping her reel in a sailfish skittering in the distance. Tucked between the bank papers was a copy of an investment questionnaire. In a wobbly hand, he'd written his desired bond and stock ratio, his timeline for retirement, eight years away, and specified that he had a low appetite for risk. At the bottom of the sheet of paper, he'd included his contact information.

"We could pick up the phone right now and call Richard Swain," I said. "I'm looking at his phone number."

"And say what?" Elise said, poking her head around the kitchen door, just in time to see me pour another pre-Christmas ration of Cutty Sark into the chipped crystal glass.

"I know what you did, Dick."

I watched Elise smile against her will and then touch her forehead, gently shaking her head as if she couldn't believe what I'd just said. But why would that be any more complicated than what had come before? Hadn't he forced us into this position by sending his hired gang to the house?

"You've got to use a lower voice," Elise said. "More calm and monotonous."

I tried it again, and for a moment she stopped smiling, as if I might actually have the balls to do this.

"Let's sleep on this one," she said, walking toward me. She held out her hand, and I gave her the glass. She took a sip, winced, and handed it back to me.

"I'm going to give you a number, Dick," I said in my blackmail voice, which had taken on a faint Eastern European accent. "And you're going to write it down very carefully."

"I'm sure he'll write it down very carefully," Elise said. But something made her stand in front of me, carefully folding a dishtowel like a small flag, waiting for me to say something else. I think she liked my Eastern European blackmail voice, as far-fetched as it was.

"Three hundred and seventy-eight thousand," I said, sliding my hand up her ribbed leggings. She gripped my wrist before I reached her thigh.

"Five hundred even," she said. "Only amateurs come up with odd numbers."

We made it look nice before we sat down. Elise found a box of tapered candles and we set them all around the dining room. We put on some thundering Bach organ chorale and added each dish to the sideboard as if we were some kind of proof. Proof of love, proof of stability, proof of a single unadulterated ordinary moment.

And then, just like he did every year, her brother called. She picked up her cell phone and immediately I could hear his voice wishing her a Merry Christmas as she walked back into the kitchen.

I turned down the stereo, just as I'd once turned down the television in Brooklyn, so I could hear Elise's end of the conversation. She was trying to keep her voice low, but I could tell she was upset about something. *You stupid shit,* she said.

Her brother spoke for a good long time, explaining something to her that I would never hear. I could hear my wife try to interrupt his monologue on the other end by repeating his name again and again, only to go on listening to whatever Ryder had to say.

I was watching her through the frosted glass of the kitchen door as she anxiously paced and shifted the phone to her other ear, and then I suddenly imagined that her own brother had molested her too. Or Victor had done something to both of them. Why would they talk to each other once a year, adhering to this one last, painful custom?

Whatever Ryder was saying to her must have reassured her because suddenly she was asking him if *he* was safe. Then it hit me. There had been no recorded voice asking her if she wanted to accept the call from the Hamilton County Jail.

I was standing to the side of the door now, the stupid platoon of violins on the stereo beginning their slow build. I tried to hear over them, but now I was just catching a word or two.

"The Hub . . . blood . . . Dick's house . . . V-Rex . . . Merry Christmas to you too."

As soon as she hung up, I pushed open the swinging door and confronted her.

"Nice of him to call," I said. "I don't know what we'd do without him."

"Not now," Elise said, pulling open the oven and shoving her hand inside a pale blue oven mitt.

"It's really too bad he can't join us out here. Share a little of the turkey this year."

"He's an inmate in Ohio," Elise said, dumping the foil-covered roasting pan on the counter. "I don't think he's going to make it."

When I get angry, my saliva feels like it's turning to acid. I could feel it stinging my throat as I tried to swallow.

"I didn't hear the voice asking you to accept the call," I said. "He's out of jail. He's not an inmate anymore."

Elise shook off the kitchen mitt and lifted the foil to take a peek at a singed turkey wing, lightly touching it with her fingers.

"He's at a halfway house in Urbana, Ohio," she said, staring at me as if I'd accosted her. "He shares a room with a sex offender and a nineteen-year-old arsonist. He's wearing an ankle bracelet. I don't think you have to worry about him, Scott. But it being Christmas, some compassion would be nice."

"Elise, I was listening," I said, moving toward her. I tried to hug her, but she ducked away. Our positions were reversed now. I was standing by the stupid turkey and she was standing by the door. "Did Ryder send those guys?"

Elise looked like she wanted to kill me. And that pissed me off. Blood isn't thicker than water. It was as simple as that.

"I'm your husband," I reminded her. "That still counts for something, right?"

"Yeah, it counts for something," she said tersely. "My brother isn't some kingpin. He's been kicked around since he was born."

Even without laying eyes on the guy, I could tell how much Elise loved him. And that pissed me off even more. If she could make that big-sister face for some loser with an ankle bracelet, where did I fit into the equation? For starters, there were going to be no more secrets. I wanted to know every petty crime the guy had committed. How they'd grown so close. Had she ever given him money? Lied for him?

"This brother thing," I said. "It's a blind spot for me. We're going to have to start from the beginning."

"There's no beginning to start from," she said. "I'm the only one he trusts. He didn't send anyone. He owes people favors. He has a big mouth and they know he's got a rich father. He sent them to the wrong house on purpose to *protect* us."

"Well, that's great," I said. "Because it's just a matter of time before they find out Victor lives eighty feet away."

"They're stupid. They didn't find anything. Believe me, they're done."

I briefly found myself picturing the guy who had nearly kicked the living shit out of me and Elise just humbly moving on to the next act of violence or extortion, wherever that might take them.

"Thank you for letting it go tonight," she said before I could say another word. "It's not exactly a world-champion family."

"V-Rex, though," I said, finally able to mention her nickname for Victor. "That's pretty apt."

I laughed a little, but she didn't join in. She waited for my mouth to straighten up again. Her refusal to let me share in this private language made me even more envious. Because how close can a couple be if they can't create their own private language? *Fuck Ryder,* I thought.

"We came up with stuff," she said, looking out the windows at the balcony, the floodlight overhead catching the cold mist coming off the water. "That's the way we coped."

With that, she turned her back on me and walked into the dining room. I stood there for a moment, and then I picked up the casserole, cursing the hot Pyrex, and brought it into the dining room.

For the rest of the evening, it was as if we'd made a silent pact not to talk about a single consequential thing. We focused on the food.

There were sweet potatoes; stuffing; cranberry jelly the way I like it, right out of the can and still ribbed by the tin; and of course the endlessly defrosted turkey.

I told her it was the juiciest turkey I'd ever tasted, even though she was right. It was bone dry. We danced around each other conversationally like we were on the fucking Wollman Rink, separated by a solid yard of vined tablecloth, decorated with real red berries she had plucked outside. I had moved on to complimenting the berries when she stopped me.

"Stop," she said, as if she were remembering something.

"All right," I said, taking another sip of wine. "But this turkey . . ."

"Shut up," she said, holding up her hand. "I thought I heard something."

We both sat there for a moment, tilting our heads.

"Is it that breathing sound?" I said.

"No."

"Because that's the pump working on the toilet. You jiggle the handle."

"It's not the toilet."

"It's the knocking," I said. "That steady faint sound of knocking?"

"Yeah," she said.

I smiled, nodded, bit my lip confidently. I knew exactly what that was. I could set her mind at peace on that subject.

After it snowed or rained, the knocking would go on for hours, and it had an odd sonic effect. It could sound like someone hammering, or chopping wood in the forest.

I told her this with pleasure, stabbing a piece of dry turkey.

"But it hasn't snowed recently," she said softly. "It hasn't rained."

I said something about a delayed leak on the roof and we both stood near the window and I showed her where the water would drip on the oak railing, but there was nothing dripping, and the sound was still there. Steady, distant, an unmistakable hammering sound, as if someone were working in pitch blackness, driving nails into a hard piece of wood. We both knew it came from the general direction of the house next door, but we never mentioned that. We slowly returned to the table, but our appetites had been ruined. After a few minutes of failing to cover up the sound with feeble conversation, we silently took our full plates back to the kitchen and scraped them into the trash. As Elise loaded up the dishwasher, I walked around the house, making sure that all the doors were locked. It didn't make me feel one bit safer.

We had hardly even celebrated New Year's, watching the ball drop on television. Out on the freezing deck, we shared a cigarette that Elise had bummed from a nurse at the hospital and watched some distant fireworks explode soundlessly across the bay. And then there was nothing but a half moon and the blinking red light of the Coast Guard antenna measuring its own steady beat. We kissed each other and she hurried back inside, leaving me with the last of the cigarette. I smoked it down to the filter, looking at the dark slope of Swain's roof, imagining the cold rooms and moonlit furniture. Then I gathered our champagne glasses from the railing and followed Elise inside.

For different reasons, we didn't sleep much that week, but I think it was a Sunday night, a couple of days after that extremely low-key New Year's, that she turned toward me in the middle of the night and announced the news.

"He wants to die at home," she said.

I had been fantasizing about blackmailing Richard Swain. Because I figured it was Richard Swain who had murdered his wife. I had all the little details nailed into place in my mind, right down to the obsolete phone booth near the supermarket I'd use to make the first call. I could even imagine the sound of his voice. The silence he'd impose on me after I mentioned the blood. Elise would be sitting in the Volvo, waiting for me, as excited as she'd been when we first trespassed into the house next door. If we were going to save our marriage, we had to keep the adrenaline going, and having her father return to die at home would derail that instantly.

"Why would he want to do that? What's wrong with the hospital?"

"Because this is his home," Elise said. "This is his bedroom. He wants to be where he feels comfortable. Not some depressing hospital."

"What can I say?" I said. "Any particular day he was thinking of making the move?"

"You're an asshole."

"I'm not," I said, reaching for her hand in the dark. She snapped it away.

"Tomorrow," she said. "I'm assuming you're willing to help. You don't have any pressing obligations?"

"I don't think so."

We lay there for a few more minutes, lost in our thoughts. I felt sure she was thinking of what it would be like at the very end for her father, and whether she'd be able to handle it.

Victor arrived, as promised, the following day, accompanied by a very pleasant home health aide named Sandra.

She was a middle-aged white woman with curly yellow hair and fleshy arms. I have this image of her, standing in the driveway in her powder-blue uniform as Victor walked away from the van that had brought him to his own home, its motorized ramp whining back into place. I can see her smiling at me a little uncertainly, because we haven't even introduced ourselves yet, and she's keeping pace with the doomed man. Victor's face is as bloodless as the bland gray sky that hangs over us and he's been dressed as if he were attempting a summit of Mount Everest instead of three steps. I can remember the elaborate pockets of a blue parka, wool hat, fur-rimmed boots, thick brown corduroys, and the forked tube that carried fresh oxygen into his nasal cavity.

My first mistake was attempting to make a joke.

"It's Sir Edmund Hillary," I said. "Welcome home."

I don't know what offended him more, the dumb joke or the fact that I had the nerve to welcome him into his own home. His forward progress, which had been glacial to begin with, completely stopped, and he swayed slightly, just enough that Sandra tightened her grip on his elbow and asked him if he was all right. His purplish lips dropped open, the way a mouth does to permit the entrance of, say, a thermometer.

It was his version of a smile, and since he could barely speak and inhale that much-needed oxygen at the same time, it was the best he could do to defend himself. I felt so sorry for him then that I think I blushed. Elise and I helped Sandra, and suddenly the three of us were slowly escorting him through the front door. It took us nearly an hour to maneuver him into his bedroom, which Elise and I had dutifully abandoned that morning, retreating to the small room that she used to share with her brother.

Sandra, bless her heart, did everything she could to make Victor comfortable. She changed channels for him, helped him eat, stood with one hand on his shoulder, encouraging him to keep on trying to shit. I know this because I was watching from a distance, amazed at what she was doing without complaint for fifteen dollars an hour. As I listened to her patiently talking to him in the bathroom, I was so moved that I decided to cancel the whole stupid blackmail scheme. I don't know what it was, exactly. Maybe some childhood memory of my own mother encouraging me as I sat in some cold bathroom, a patience tender beyond words. The moments I feel ashamed are always triggered by something embarrassingly specific.

Besides, I no longer pictured Richard Swain standing next to his mistress on a boat in the Florida Keys. That was too easy. My best guess was that he had put his terminally ill wife out of her misery and shot her point-blank as she slept, right there on that bed, and then he had fled. How craven would it be to pick up a phone and torture him now, especially with another terminally ill man squatting in a bathroom a few feet away from me?

There would be other ways for Elise and I to save our marriage. At some point in the spring, or by Memorial Day at least, her father would cease to exist, her brother would do something stupid and be tucked away in Hamilton County again, and by Christmas, next Christmas, we'd be holding hands and drinking spiked eggnog in front of our friends, and if I couldn't get Elise pregnant again, we'd adopt some incredible, loving child from Moldavia, or Peru.

I wanted to share this almost manic cascade of thoughts with Elise, but she was busy in the kitchen, sprinkling 4C bread crumbs on a casserole, so I thought I should let her be.

Later that night, Sandra's husband came to pick her up. It must have been around ten o'clock. I thanked her for putting up with Victor.

"You're not getting rid of me that fast," she said, laughing. "I'm going to see you all bright and early tomorrow."

It's very hard for me, even now, to recall those words. Of course, she did come back, bright and early. She tended patiently to Victor in the bedroom he had picked for his big exit, softly singing some old song that repeated the same words over and over again until he suddenly barked at her to stop.

I don't want to be easy on myself. It's always simple to slide away from your own selfishness in a marriage. I mean my marriage. I can think of all the opportunities I had to say something wonderful, or to touch Elise in a certain way.

I could have kissed her neck as she stood by the kitchen counter, reading the pharmacy warnings that came stapled to Victor's opiates. I could have wrapped my arms around her waist, but I didn't because I thought it was too great a risk at the time. She hadn't slept the night before and she'd polished off almost a full bottle of red wine. It's painful when I see myself just glide by her, stand just two feet away from her and crimp fucking aluminum foil around a half-eaten casserole.

I could have told her how much I loved her many times that night, but instead I played it cool, leaving her alone with her thoughts, asking her once, I think, if she had any objection to me running the dishwasher.

"Why would I have any objection?" she said, pouring herself another glass of wine.

Her back is to me, light from the lamp above her head shining down on the furrow in her neck. Her black hair pulled back. I distinctly remember being aware of the fact that she was wearing her good earrings, the sapphires I'd bought her a few years before. I think she had put them on to look nice for her father, who, of course, had probably never noticed.

We didn't argue that night. She told me that she was going to check on her father and that it didn't matter if I ran the dishwasher because he'd be too zonked on morphine and wouldn't hear anything anyway.

She stood by the kitchen door, one hand starting to push it open, eyes cast downward. Of all the things that are painful about that night, the most is the realization I have, even now, of how tired she was of everything, but most of all, of me. There is nothing I can do to change her expression when she finally looked up at me. Elise could let you know how she felt by just frowning slightly or turning her head away.

I cannot lie to you and say that I knew beyond a doubt we were still meant for each other. I realized our relationship probably sustained fatal damage around the time of the miscarriage, but there aren't any breaking headlines when it comes to a marriage. No one's going to arrest you for giving it another week, another month. When she looked back at me, by the kitchen door, all I saw was doubt. It had only grown since I left her in the woods, making my own escape. If her father hadn't come home, I think she might have left me in January.

"Been a long day," she said. "Maybe tomorrow will be better."

I poured some Cascade into the dispenser and thought about how I could sum up our bright future in a few words.

"It's just a rough patch," I said, looking up, but she was already gone. Only one thing was out of the ordinary. She had left her phone on the kitchen table. I could see that a new text had arrived, and even though I didn't know how to unlock her phone, I could read it on the screen.

"on my way :)" it said. And above it, a telephone number I didn't recognize.

I could feel the anger tightening my larynx, and the muscles along my spine seizing up. Pushing open the front door, I stepped outside and listened to some unseen bird flap away in the darkness. Then, carefully re-tapping the number into the keypad of my cell phone, I sat on the cold wood of the front step, waited, and got a voicemail. I knew that voice.

"The only people for me are the mad ones," the pompous voice breathed, more than spoke. "If you're normal don't even bother leaving a message."

I hung up. Curt Page. I wondered how this jerk would look ten years after we'd kicked him out of the loft. Curt Page, freshly divorced and apparently headed toward the East Coast.

I called again, waited for the beep, and tried to keep my voice steady.

"Hi, Curt," I said. "It's your old buddy Scott. If you ever text my wife again I'm going to fucking kill you."

No, that wasn't specific enough, I thought, bubbles of anger rising up painfully in my chest. I thought of the shotgun in Victor's closet.

"I'm going to stick a shotgun in your mouth and blow off

the back of your head. Do you understand me? How's your fucking novel going?"

His voicemail did not object to the tone of my voice. Three more times I called back, asking him in a constipated whisper: *Do you understand me? Do you understand me? Do you?*

Then I sat there, the screens of both phones eventually extinguishing themselves and leaving me on the dark step, listening to the small, breaking waves of the bay down below. I felt alone and frantic for a moment, until I saw the upstairs light switch on in the house next door. I knew it was just some automatic system, but the light felt vaguely comforting, even as faint as it was. Just a plain white rectangle partly hidden from view every time the pines were stirred by the wind.

A fifth of Jack Daniel's was the best of the second-tier hard stuff left in Victor's liquor cabinet. I'd finished off the Bacardi, Sauza, Dewar's, Pernod, Hennessy, Cutty Sark, and Smirnoff. Only the Jack Daniel's and a bottle of sweet vermouth remained. I poured some bourbon into one of Victor's chipped mugs. I poured Victor one too, and I carried my offering into the bedroom that, until that night, I'd somehow thought of as mine.

Victor was watching the military channel from his bed, his index finger loosely pinching the oxygen tube that led to his nose. There was a steady *pssshhh* every time the oxygen released from its canister on the side of the bed. He didn't turn toward me as I walked into the room.

"I brought you a little nightcap," I said, putting the mug down on the nightstand. I sat on the chair next to his bed and briefly glanced at the television before tuning in to his face. I sipped the bourbon and studied the drifting television phosphorescence that crept back and forth on his waxy forehead. His jaw had dropped open and the only reason I knew he wasn't dead was because once or twice his tongue slid along his bottom lip and glinted in the light. His breathing already seemed highly irregular. His chest didn't seem to move for minutes on end, and then it would suddenly heave. Needless to say, he never touched the bourbon I'd brought him.

I don't know why, but I had a surge of sympathy that makes me cringe now. I leaned over and squeezed his slightly cold foot. He flicked his pale blue eyes downward as if I were touching someone else's extremity. It made the sensation of touching him even stranger. The fact that his foot felt like cold marble underneath the sock didn't exactly help, and I was more than happy to withdraw my fingers.

It's funny how seamlessly the last subject came up. Through the blinds I could see that the lights were on in the house next door. For a moment, I considered telling Victor everything. If there was one person I could confess to, it would be a guy on the way out. Maybe he even knew a thing or two about Richard Swain, having lived right next to him for a number of years. What I decided to share with him, instead, was my uncanny knowledge of the future. I waited a few more minutes, till the green digits on the nightstand's alarm clock read 10:59, and then I told him what was going to happen.

"Those lights are going to switch off in a minute," I said, pointing at the house next door. "It's always the same."

This time, Victor turned to me with real interest, and when he spoke, it startled me.

"I own that house," he said.

I sank back in the chair, watching him watch me. He pinched the tube again, as if he wanted to see what would happen if he interrupted the steady stream. It made him wince slightly and raise his chin. He let go and slid one hand along the bedspread. I decided to let the subject drop. I had seen the warnings on the opiates and was pretty sure he didn't fully comprehend anything.

"You don't believe me?" he said.

I still would have let it go, but the corners of his mouth had risen in an unpleasant, taunting way, so I thought, even considering the circumstances, it would be appropriate to set him straight.

"Belongs to a guy named Dick Swain," I said. "He hasn't been around for some time."

Victor waited for a *pssshhh* of oxygen to vent into his larynx and then he got back to this final business.

"I purchased it from Dick Swain in 2011," he said.

He barely got to the end of the sentence. Anything over four words seemed to put him into agony. But having imparted this information to me, I could tell that he was pleased.

"Does Elise know that?" I said.

"Of course," he said.

"She would have told me," I said. I was trying to keep calm, though I felt the back of my neck getting hot, and cold, and hot again. It was like someone had just told me he'd spotted Elise with another man. My wife, with her secrets, kept slipping away from me. I blamed it on this prick in front of me. He was the one who'd taught her to keep secrets as a child, and now they were spreading. I'd make her write a list of all of them later. We'd get to the bottom of it. The last one. How bad could the worst one be?

"She wouldn't have told you," he said, as if he'd always know more about my wife than I could ever hope to understand. "I made her promise."

I stared at him and tried to think of how I could surprise him, just enough to let him know I wasn't as predictable as he thought.

"We broke in the other night," I said.

He turned and faced the ceiling. Looking pleased, he asked me to tell him more.

"There's blood on a mattress in there. Someone got killed. What do you know about that?"

It was my final move. For a moment I thought I'd gained a little ground back, but when he turned to me again, he had a strange look of pleasure on his face, the crease in his forehead completely smoothed out. He continued sliding the bunched knuckles of his left hand down the bedspread until he grasped the remote control. I watched his thumb writhe over the tiny buttons until, just by luck, he was able to turn the television off, throwing us into complete darkness. Complete except for the lights on the timer that was still on.

I couldn't tell if Victor was watching me or the lighted window, but at 11:00, just as I had promised, the house next door fell dark. There wasn't a sound in the bedroom until the oxygen tank released its miserly *pssshhh* again. Victor spoke to me as he began to sink into a morphined sleep.

"Why don't you take your turn with her?"

"With who?" I said.

"Carmelita. She's waiting for you in the basement."

I asked him what he was talking about and then I remembered the voicemail. Victor's voice telling Carmelita he was worried about her.

"I recommend you do it in front of the mirrors. I moved them in front of the fireplace so I could watch."

"Who's Carmelita?"

"The winter girl," he said, drifting off. "Everyone should have a winter girl."

12

Of course, I wished it were a joke. But even if the girl Victor was talking about existed, she would be long gone. The idea of some naked, freezing creature scurrying from room to room in the house next door disturbed me for a moment, until I wrote it off as impossible. Or maybe it was a fantasy he'd come up with some night, after drinking too much by himself in his study. Maybe it was some woman from his past he'd tried to call. I could picture him drunkenly dialing Swain's number instead. After Victor's cancer diagnosis, Elise had told me he was hitting the booze and sleeping pills heavily every night, unable to get to sleep.

But I didn't entirely write it off. I stood by the bedroom window after Elise had fallen asleep and watched the lights in the house next door come on, spooking myself when I thought I saw something move in one of the upstairs bedrooms in Swain's house. But it was nothing, just reflections of the bare branches in the gully between the houses, moving with the wind. I don't remember exactly what time it was when I finally pulled the covers back and lay down next to Elise, but I could feel the resentment building again. I hated the fact that Victor thought I could be so easily taken advantage of. And what did he expect me to do with this little bit of news? Lure this phantom creature from her hiding place with a plate of hot food and warm clothes?

And then there was the matter of Curt Page and the text. I shook Elise awake. It's funny how I could immediately tell she was awake. She sucked in a long breath through her nose and then expelled it slowly.

"What?" she said.

"Curt Page says he's on his way."

"You talked to him?"

"He texted you."

"When?"

"About thirty minutes ago. I called him back, got his voicemail."

She turned away from me again, pulled the covers up to her shoulders.

"Don't worry about Curt Page," she said. "I never respond to him."

I thought that sounded strange. Was there someone I should worry about?

"What's going on, Elise? You're getting weird Christmas calls from your brother. Curt thinks he's on a pilgrimage to you. And your father just told me something even more ridiculous."

I was going to tell her about the winter girl who Victor had highly recommended having, but Elise cut me off.

"You've been drinking," she said. "I can hear it in your voice."

"Of course I've been drinking. Things are getting a little disturbing, to be quite honest."

Short of slurring, being overly formal was the surest tip-off to Elise that I was too drunk to waste time on. *Quite honest.*

"Quite honestly," she said, still turned away from me, "you're the one who's starting to disturb me the most. I need support more than you do right now. My dad is dying downstairs."

He was actually watching the military channel, I wanted to tell her, and trying to arouse me with lurid delusions about a strange girl there to service whoever found her. But before I could provide this information, I could hear Elise lightly snoring.

I dreamed of her, the winter girl, that night. Her whitish lips and expressionless oval face, layered in Martha and Richard Swain's scavenged clothes. Her fingers stretched out from the cuff of an old parka, and I stood there, as you would before some timid animal, waiting for her to touch my cheek.

In the morning, I found myself standing at the kitchen sink, squinting at the silvery light on Shinnecock Bay. Elise was still asleep upstairs, taking advantage of one of the few perks of having Victor back home. At least she didn't have to slog out to the car to visit him in the hospital.

I was making her a breakfast tray, scraping some butter on a piece of toast and carefully placing a chipped cream pourer on the tray, when I heard Victor's distinctive hacking cough coming from his bedroom.

Forcing myself to take a deep sigh, I walked down the hallway, tray in hand, and checked on him. He was sitting upright in bed, hacking into Kleenex he had balled up in his fist.

"What have you brought me?" he said hoarsely, staring at the tray.

"It's for Elise," I said, taking another step toward the bed. It was amazing how his face, drier than the knotted bedroom carpet, took on the exact color of the light outside. His eyes weren't exactly glittering with new life, but they were wet enough from the coughing to shine.

"I have a message for her," he said, taking no interest in

the steaming coffee cup on the tray. He preferred to stare at the window.

"Why don't you write it on a piece of paper and I'll take it up to her."

"I'm not talking about my daughter," Victor said, the bottom half of his face flinching in annoyance. "The girl. My winter girl."

"Sure," I said, indulging him for the moment. "What would you like me to say to her?"

"Tell her the truth," he said, extending one of his thin fingers to delicately scratch the stubble on the side of his neck. "Tell her I nearly died. Tell her I'm back from the dead."

"First item on my list of things to do today," I said, bowing my head sarcastically. "Right after I take a crap and brush my teeth."

I was about to leave him in his sordid fantasyland when he reached for something underneath his pillow. It was an envelope, filled with some carefully smoothed-out cash, and on it was scrawled CARMELITA.

"Five hundred and six dollars," he said. "I counted it twice. I want you to bring it to her."

Sure thing, I thought to myself, a little taken aback that this fantasy project of Victor's actually had a name. That was a nice touch. He'd probably get a real kick out of this if I really fell for it and wandered around Swain's house shouting this name. It didn't matter. The money was mine now anyway.

"You're a big spender," I said.

"Can't give them too much," he said, watching me fold the envelope in half and stuff it in the back pocket of my jeans. "Just enough to keep them interested."

I picked up the tray again and started to leave the room, even though he was calling my name, determined to give me more advice about this phantom he had invented.

"Get some rest, Victor," I said. "You sound like you really need it."

F*ive hundred and six bucks,* I thought, spitting out toothpaste. In the bathroom mirror, I could see part of the bed. Elise's body still bunched up under the comforter, snoring softly again. She'd wake herself up, stare blankly around the room, and fall asleep again. I'd left the tray on the small desk, the coffee already gone cold.

I spat again and walked back into the bedroom, my feet bare and cold. I pulled out a dresser drawer and Elise opened her eyes again.

"You brought me breakfast," she said. "That's sweet of you."

Fishing two mismatched socks out of the drawer, I sat on the edge of the bed and pulled them on. Then I stepped into my permanently laced sneakers and reached out toward her, grabbing her hand.

I was going to tell her about her father's five hundred and six dollars and this winter girl he wanted me to pay off in Swain's house, but she'd closed her eyes again.

I swear I was going to tell her.

The weather changed fast in Shinnecock Hills. You could be blinking at the cold bright sun one moment and then watching ash-colored clouds thicken over the inlet. The light that had glittered across the bay just an hour before had been replaced by a dense fog that drifted westward from the ocean. The sky and bay had melted into the same grayness and only the branches of the nearest trees could be seen.

I opened the door that led to Victor's deck, navigated myself around a few insistent scabs of ice and then down the back stairs. I climbed over the fence and found the deer path. The red berries suspended in the underbrush even had a grayish tint. I thought I could smell the fog as I moved through it. It had the faint odor of wet cement. It crept down the black path like dry ice, and as I made my way around the empty pool I had that sense of myself walking into a scene again, as if the empty house and everything in it had been constructed just for me.

Almost two weeks had passed since the sliding glass door had been kicked in, and it still had not been repaired, though the shattered bits of glass were harder to see in the flat light. Gusts of rain, snow, dew, had claimed some of the furniture in the living room. The back of the yellow sofa was streaked with water. A lampshade was ruined, a finger of moisture beginning to split its only seam. A seagull or crow had briefly made a tour of the place, leaving a whitish pile of birdshit near the ficus tree. The only difference between this visit and the previous ones was that I was carrying an envelope filled with cash.

I cringed as I did just what Victor wanted me to do.

"Carmelita!" I shouted.

I wandered into the downstairs bedroom, pulled open one of the folding closets, stared up at some blankets on a shelf, and called her name again, just for the hell of it.

Nothing. Just the daylight in the house fading for a moment as the fog continued to roll in. I got down on my knees, looked under the bed, imagining her cowering there.

"Hey, Carmelita," I said, walking back into the living room. Above me, the useless chandelier and all its gaudy crystal pendants. The cream-colored carpet running all the way up the staircase. The array of abandoned liqueurs on the teak cabinet. *Crème de menthe,* I thought to myself, trying to unscrew its crusty cap. *Who even drinks this stuff anymore?*

"Hey, Carmelita," I said again, finally twisting open the bottle and taking a sickening, minty sip. "I've got your money. Five hundred and six bucks. Victor says he counted it twice."

There's nothing more depressing than talking to yourself while drinking crème de menthe. So I picked up an ancient-looking bottle of Cointreau, wrestled its gluey cork out, and took a longer sip. In the distance, I could see the fog doubling down, erasing the long-necked black birds that roosted on the dock, one by one.

"Who are you?" a voice said from the top of the staircase. I swung around and took a few steps back.

She was a frightened-looking Hispanic girl, with black hair that fell to her shoulders. She was wearing jeans and a faded red sweatshirt. I'll tell you right away, she wasn't a knockout. You might pass her on the street without a second look, but here, in an empty house, it was another story. Everything took on more weight, even the way she tucked a strand of her hair behind her ear and then nervously folded and unfolded her arms. At least she had the advantage of talking to me from above, one knee tucked between the brass railings.

"My name is Scott," I said, holding up the envelope as if it were evidence of my good intentions. I was just a courier, after all. "Victor's my father-in-law."

This information did nothing to ease the tension. She seemed to be summing me up, pursing her lips and gripping the railing now with one hand. You notice little things at first when you're just getting to know someone. The pink polish on her fingernails had chipped off, and there were three dark scabs on her wrist. She wasn't anything like the winter girl I had seen in my dreams. First of all, she seemed to be wearing her own clothes, right down to the Day-Glo orange Nikes she tapped against the railing.

"Were you here the whole time?" I shouted up at her. "When I was walking around with my wife? When those guys broke in?"

Walking around is a mild way of putting it, I chided myself.

There was sex, then the discovery of the blood on the sheets, then Elise throwing up all over the bedroom.

"I was hiding in the basement," Carmelita said softly, sweeping her hair behind her ear again and then turning toward the staircase. "There's a narrow space behind the boiler. It would be murder if the heat worked, but the metal is ice cold now."

She took a few steps downward and then paused, gripping the railing again to get a closer look at me. And, of course, I got a better look at her: no makeup, brown eyes, a slight build. I stared back at her face, just to let her know I wasn't another version of Victor, some scumbag who thought he could pay her to do anything he wanted.

"Anyway," I said, slowly walking toward her and reaching up to hand her the envelope. "This is yours."

That should have been the end of our entire interaction. I should have turned around, walked right back out onto the ruined patio that faced the sea, and immediately divulged everything to Elise.

Instead I watched her open the envelope and count the twenties Victor had carefully placed inside and then the five-dollar bill and the stingy buck, added like a specific insult. As she counted the money, I could clearly see that her nose was misshapen, probably broken, and that there was the faintest trace of purple under both eyes, a sliver of it suspended underneath the skin, but still visible in that light.

She didn't continue walking down the stairs; she sat down, folding the envelope in two and then four before stuffing it into her pocket. She made a snuffling sound with her nose and I took another step closer, ready to comfort her, until I saw that she wasn't crying. I watched her wipe her sleeve against her runny nose and then, for the first time, she smiled.

"This is fucked up," she said.

There are some people who can smile and you wish you could send them back to the happiness shop: my old boss, for instance, Chuck Meyer, at the New School, who looked like he was rising out of a coffin every time he cracked a joke, his thin red lips stretching back on his unusually small teeth. But Carmelita had a smile that changed everything about her face. It went right to her flashing brown eyes, then back down to her lips, making them purse in a way that seemed more innocent than sarcastic. I'd only just met her and I didn't feel wary at all. In my dream, the stranger had reached out to touch my face with cold fingers, but when I finally made the silly gesture of shaking Carmelita's hand, her fingers were warm, her handshake polite, before she pulled her arm away and folded her arms again.

"It is fucked up," I said, glancing quickly at the sliding glass door, just to make sure Elise hadn't followed me there. Was she even still asleep? Or was Victor handing her another envelope for Carmelita so that she could find me here? It didn't matter. I'd tell her everything as soon as I got back to the house.

"I thought he was dead," she said, her smile vanishing. She was sizing me up again. "I was relieved. No one was going to bother me for the rest of the winter."

"What are you doing here?" I said.

"I worked for Richard Swain," she said. "He was a nice guy. His wife was sick. Brain tumor. He spent everything he had on doctors. He was losing his mind a little too. He didn't even ask for the house key when he let me go. He was going to travel to Lake Geneva with her. There was a doctor there who said he could keep her alive for another three months."

She reached into her pocket and took out a single house key on a rusty ring.

"So I came by this summer. I thought at least he'd be

back," she said. "But I don't know where he is. Maybe he's dead. He told me he had no interest in living after she was gone."

The image of Richard Swain changed in my mind again. I could picture him over his dying wife in an ornate hotel room on Lake Geneva. The rasp of her breathing. Her grayish eyes open but unfocused. Carmelita pocketed the key again.

"Maybe he'll surprise us," I said.

"No," she said. "Victor's the only one who noses around. For weeks he didn't even have the guts to let himself in. He's a coward, you know. I watched him sneaking around, pretending he was just a normal guy when he heard a car on the road. He would put his hands on his hips and try to look like he was interested in the house."

"That sounds about right. I can see that."

That didn't earn any points with her—the fact that I could sympathize. I had the feeling that others had tried that route, and it disgusted her now. She wrote it off and simply moved on to the next subject.

"So I have a useless house key and some cash from an old man. Maybe there are worse things."

I told her there were. I cleared my throat. I told her I should be getting back to my house. I meant Victor's house. We both didn't belong where we happened to exist at that moment. So it was hard to establish an official way to say goodbye.

"I'll hit him up for some more cash," I said, backing away. "If that helps."

She didn't say a word. She just smiled quickly. Stood up and watched me step outside. She knew I'd be back.

When I got back to Victor's home, I made sure to walk around the back side of the house. I picked up a cold mug of coffee I had left on the deck and stood there admiring the lifting fog. Elise, wrapped tight in a terry-cloth bathrobe, her hair still wet from the shower, joined me out there.

"Give me a sip," she said, reaching for the mug. I handed it to her and she made a face as she drank.

"Sorry," I said. "I let it get cold."

"How long have you been standing out here?"

"I don't know. Half an hour? I didn't want to wake you up."

I was waiting for the right moment to tell her exactly what I was doing and what her father had been up to. Then it occurred to me that there would be a very good chance that Elise would be furious, tearing downstairs to confront her father, and then even the girl next door. But there was another reason I held my tongue. I needed more information. At least one more visit with Carmelita to find out exactly what had been going on.

I could hear the sound of a car's tires on the gravel driveway and then the slamming of a door. Sandra, Victor's home health aide, had arrived.

"Saint Sandra is here," Elise said, tossing the coffee on the brown grass below. "Want to hear something disgusting?"

"Sure," I said, squinting at the sunlight that had suddenly begun to fall everywhere. A slab of white light thrown across Elise, making her wet hair gleam. "Does it involve Victor?"

"Who else? I walked by the bedroom yesterday and saw him squeeze her thigh. Sandra slapped his hand right off and he would've tried it again if he hadn't seen me."

"No shame. He should really be forced to live in a giant glass box with a heat lamp and a rock."

Elise smiled at that, the thought of her father as a giant reptile, walled off for good.

"You know what the funny thing is?" Elise said, picking up the empty coffee cup and hurling it as far as she could. I listened to a distant thump as it landed on the sandy hill. "He's getting better."

"No, he's not," I said, a little taken aback by her annihilation of the coffee cup.

He wasn't getting better. I'd heard him sucking harder on his oxygen, I'd listened to the coughing fits. The man had bedsores. He was losing weight. His eyes were glistening and faintly yellow. Two nights ago he had awakened early in the morning, screaming for his pain medication, and then his hydrocodone. The doctor had assured us that he had three months to live, and that was six months ago, just before they checked him in.

"Maybe it's being back home," Elise said. "Maybe the doctor was wrong."

"We saw X rays. It's all over the place. It's in his lungs. His bladder. He's barely hanging in there."

Elise shrugged and then turned away, opening the screen door that led directly to our bedroom. I stayed out on the second-floor deck, watching her let the bathrobe fall to the floor and then walk to the mirror over the dresser, frowning at herself as she picked up a hairbrush and plucked away some strands in its pins. If it had been any other day, I would have played the part of the intruder, slipping in and dragging her to the bed, fucking loudly enough so that Victor and Sandra could hear us downstairs.

But I was looking at the house next door, and then not just looking, but also shielding my eyes against the sun, wondering if Carmelita had been watching us from one of the blistered windows of Swain's home, trying to guess what I had been confessing to my wife. When I glanced back at the bedroom, Elise, to my surprise, had turned around again, pulling on a pair of jeans and balancing on one leg. She grabbed her bra from the chair and walked toward the screen door, pressing her face against it.

"Don't even think about that house again," she said. "We've got plenty to deal with over here."

"Promise," I said, opening the door and giving her a kiss on the cheek as I passed her. Downstairs, I could hear Victor having one of his epic coughing fits, followed by him cursing at Sandra, as if she were responsible. I couldn't hear how she comforted him or see what she was doing, but almost magically there wasn't another sound.

"We should really fire her," Elise said, pulling on her turtleneck and looking at herself sideways in the mirror again.

I told Elise I was going to take a walk down by the water and clear my head. She was busy making some calls in the kitchen, trying to keep up with her old contacts in the city. There was a speech rehab center in Mastic that one of her colleagues had recommended, and when I left the house she was joking about the name of the town.

"I'll take anything that'll get me out of the house," she said, tapping the end of a pen against a piece of paper she had scrawled a handful of numbers on. "Thanks, Debbie."

I was walking down the driveway, with the idea of looping around by the small beach and then climbing the ruined wooden staircase that led to Swain's home.

"Scott," Elise said, following me to the entrance of the driveway. She was holding my Nikon in her hand. I stood there as she placed the strap over my head and gave me a quick kiss. "Take some pictures at least. We've got to remember who we are, otherwise our brains are going to rot."

I could feel the heat rising in my face as she turned and walked back to the house, but not before facing me one more time and shouting out one last wish.

"Take a photo that will change our lives," she said, smirking playfully. "It can't be that hard."

It was low tide around noontime, the water in the bay slack and unrippled, brown islands of rubbery seaweed plainly visible underneath. In the distance I could see that the two duck-hunting blinds were still set up, two small thatch houses on a wooden float, about five hundred yards apart. I raised the camera to my eye and zoomed in on one of them, surprised when I saw a small skiff docked next to it, and then a stream of blue smoke from a cigarette. I couldn't see the person's face, but from the way the right side of the float dipped into the water, I figured he must be overweight and fat-fingered, snug in a red-and-black checkered hunting jacket.

I took the photo just to check the light, and then I continued up the beach. Though the fog had lifted and the sun was visible, it was still just a few degrees above freezing. As I walked parallel to Swain's home, I suddenly felt a sense of dread, as if I were willingly about to commit a terrible mistake.

And the choice was simple: I could walk right back to Victor's house and wait for my wife to finish setting up the interview. I could take her to a movie in town, then have lunch at that seafood shack on the canal and watch the fishing boats go by. Or I could risk breaking my neck by walking up a crooked row of splintered wooden steps that led to Swain's home. It looked more like a broken ladder than a staircase anyway, and to even reach the bottom step I'd have to clamber up a sandy dune and then lift myself up. And for what? Carmelita and her five hundred and six dollars would be long gone.

Decision made, I told myself, walking back toward Victor's house. I was that close to putting it all to rest when I thought I saw something move out of the corner of my eye. I glanced to my left, at the sun-smeared windows of Swain's home, and saw her looking at me. It was only movement I could see; not even her face. I knew only that she had been there, watching me, and now she wasn't.

For a long time, we said nothing. I sat on the far end of Swain's dusty-smelling couch and Carmelita sat at the other, her arms around her knees. I fiddled with the dial on the Nikon and told myself it was definitely time to leave. She hadn't exactly greeted me with a smile when she opened the sliding door. It was funny how I had waited for her to let me in, even though I could have barged right in myself. An opaque layer of plastic sheeting had been stretched across the broken glass of the sliding door and fastened there with duct tape. An ad hoc repair I thought wouldn't last past the first wind gust. We both had the same rights to be in that house, which is to say none at all.

"No envelope from Victor today?" she said, tilting her head to the side.

"No, I'm sorry," I said. "I mean, I could ask him for more."

She let that offer hang in the air for a bit, and then she leaned over and reached for my camera.

"What kind of pictures do you take?" she said.

"Brides. Mostly weddings. A lot of Asian couples. Some bar mitzvahs. Out here, though, nothing much."

She had turned the camera on but was looking up at me quizzically, not understanding how to browse through the recent photographs with the viewfinder. I moved closer to her, realizing, as my shoulder touched hers, that I was crossing another small line. Seeing myself as an amateurish adulterer, I moved away from her again and watched her scan through the photographs. My attempts at bringing out the best of Shinnecock Bay hardly registered on her face.

"I like the one of the long black bird," she said. Then she corrected herself, staring at the camera. "Its shadow."

"Yeah," I said, disgusted with myself. "I really pushed the envelope there. Bird pooping on a dock."

She laughed and gently handed the camera back to me. As she did, the sleeve stretched back on her right arm and I could see the reddish scabs again.

"You burned yourself?" I asked.

Her face flushed, but for only a few seconds; the redness around the nape of her neck quickly vanished as she pulled her sleeve back down around her wrist.

"One day I sat there and he tied me up," she said, nodding at an ornate ivory chair.

"Victor?" I said.

She nodded and told me the rest in a detached voice, as if the facts hardly mattered anymore.

"Sometimes he burns me, sometimes he bites."

She coughed out a laugh and covered her face with her hand, her fingers splayed across her nose and eyes. It was as if she were watching Victor kneel before her as she sat in the chair and begin to go to work on her.

"Fucking scumbag," I said, nervously fiddling with the camera dial again. I took off the lens cap and popped it back on.

"When I fell over in the chair, I got the tape off my hands and freed myself," she said. "He came over with the flashlight later. He took half the cash from the envelope and told me he was disappointed. He told me he'd have to come up with a better system."

"He wanted you to just lie there and suffer?"

"It's a game," she said, looking at me warily. "He pays me for it. And I get to stay here the rest of the winter. It was all right until you got curious about the house."

"So Victor owns this now," I said, prying a little. "He said he bought it from the Swains."

"He didn't have to buy anything. Richard Swain shot his wife in the bedroom downstairs. She was dying and he'd fallen in love with someone else anyway. He ran away and left everything just like this."

"You said he took her to Lake Geneva and he told you he couldn't live without her."

"No, I didn't," she said defensively. "And what if I did? All I know is that I'm here."

I needed her to straighten out her story. Had Victor told her several outcomes and was she screwing them up on purpose to get back at him? I could tell she was angry I was pressing her about this missing couple. I was suddenly worried she had never worked for them at all. I wanted to ask her how much she had made an hour, what time the Swains retired for the night, whether they watched television or sat side by side on this couch reading books by the fire. Who had written THE BEST IS YET TO COME on the grinning pig's chalkboard?

Carmelita quickly wiped her runny nose with the sleeve of her sweatshirt and stared at me.

"Martha Swain died here is all I know," Carmelita said. "Victor says he knows where Richard Swain buried her."

"Then he's an accomplice. Tell you what," I said, picturing Victor squeezing Sandra's thigh as she rubbed lotion on his withered legs. "You want him to pay you double? Triple? It's going to be even easier now."

He would pay, somehow. I told Carmelita to roll her sleeve back, just to show me the burns. She hesitated, but then she let me see her forearm and I stood over it, camera pressed to my face like some kind of evidence technician. She stood up, and as I was checking the photo of the arm, she unzipped her sweatshirt, then crossed her arms and pulled off her shirt.

I stood there for a moment, first stunned that she was half naked, and then sickened by the precise blue and dull orange bite marks around her small breasts, as if some insane suckling child had tried to tear away her dark nipples. Near her waist, there were three more distinct bites, one so deep that it had completely discolored the skin near her left hip, turning it black. I imagined her sitting in a chair, screaming, the rattling sound the chair's thin ivory legs made on the floor as he sank his yellow incisors into her.

I crouched and took photographs as she turned, bracing myself as she showed me her back, but surprisingly the skin was unbroken, except for the loose collar of bruises around her neck. I moved closer and focused on the skin there, the semicircles left by his fingers.

"Show's over, mister," she said in a fake childish voice, smiling as she pulled the shirt back over her shoulders and zipped up the sweatshirt. She didn't sit back down on the couch. I had the distinct impression she wanted me to leave.

"I'll get you some more money," I said. "Or at least I'll try."

"Give him a kiss for me," she said, turning her back to me. She reached for the banister, and I watched her soundlessly climb up the staircase and disappear into one of the bedrooms.

"I'm leaving," I said, but I just stood there for a few more minutes, wondering if she screamed or held it all in as he went at it.

14

"Any good shots?" Elise said, folding a pair of Victor's gray sweatpants as she did laundry upstairs. She chucked them in a plastic basket and slammed the dryer door closed.

"Just the usual," I said, standing in the doorway and watching her. I was weighing how I should tell her about Carmelita. Then Elise slammed the stubborn door of the dryer as it drifted open again, and I thought there might be a better time.

"He made Sandra sing," she said, brushing past me with the basket and walking downstairs. I followed her. "Some lilting Polish lullaby. Now she's making him goulash or something."

As I trailed Elise downstairs to Victor's bedroom, I could smell the onions being sautéed and Sandra still humming to herself in the kitchen. Elise pushed the door open and marched into the room with the laundry basket, ignoring her father. He was sitting upright in bed, wearing an olive-colored shirt with one quilted shoulder. It was part of an old hunting outfit.

"Going to shoot some quail?" I said, sitting on the empty twin bed.

"It's all that was left in the drawer," he said tersely. "Before this one had the bright idea to actually lift a finger."

This one, my wife, opened a dresser drawer and chucked in his sweatpants, velour leisurewear, socks, and a pile of underwear.

"How are you feeling today, Victor?" I said. "You look like you have more energy."

Any direct question from me always met with the same glittering stare. He considered me for a few seconds, trying to gauge whether I'd followed up on his tip from the night before.

Elise slammed the drawer, placed the laundry basket on top of the dresser, and left the room. I waited until I heard her asking Sandra something in the kitchen, and then I switched the camera on.

"I took some interesting shots today," I said, standing up and crossing over to his bed. It was strange sitting down next to him. He seemed to have an intense reaction to my physical proximity, lifting up his legs until they formed a tent under the sheet and taking in a deep breath, as if he were about to swim a length underwater.

"You gave her the money?"

"Yeah," I said, angling the camera toward him so that he could see the photograph I had selected. The one of Carmelita's bruised chest.

"I can't see anything in this light. What are you showing me?"

"People go to jail for this, Victor. It's called torture."

"Finally," he said, his thin blue lips rolling up until I could see his teeth. It was as if his mouth were being pulled back by invisible wires. "You have some purpose. Something to wake up for."

He never really finished the sentence because my hand was around his neck. I wasn't going to strangle him, but it must have looked that way to Sandra. She was standing in the doorway with a small red tray in her thick arms. His goulash was ready.

"Scott!" she shouted at me, putting the tray down on the bed and grabbing at my arm, even though I was already letting go. Victor's spit covered my thumb. He was doing his best to look like I was completely psychotic, coughing and turning blue as I stood up again, the camera around my neck.

"It's all right, Sandra," he said, cooing at her as if she were some loyal protective pet. "He's harmless, absolutely harmless. There's nothing to him."

I glanced at him one more time before I left the room. In her rush to rearrange his contorted body, Sandra had knocked over his array of pill bottles. They rolled in all directions on the carpet, one thin container coming to a rest underneath the curtain, where I hoped it might always be forgotten. On the way out, unseen and harmless, I cleared my throat and spat in his steaming soup.

I could hear Sandra's thumping footsteps as she followed me out of the room. She shouted my name as I entered the kitchen, still filled with the cloying smell of the goulash. A pale lump of leftover macaroni sat in a colander next to the sink.

When I turned toward Sandra, her face was contorted and red. She picked away a strand of blond hair from her perspiring forehead. I felt sorry for her, of course, not the sadistic prick in the other room.

"You were killing him," she spat out, keeping her distance from me.

"I lost my patience," I said softly. "I was actually trying to help him sit up in bed. You know how difficult he can be."

She didn't buy that. I could tell that much right away. I

watched her turn toward the portable phone and immediately pictured her picking it up and dialing the police.

"I'd love some goulash," I said, in a voice so plaintive it even surprised me. "I'm starving."

Her back was still turned, and I could sense that she was still sizing me up. Was I a generally trustworthy person who'd just lost it? Would I have finished Victor off if she hadn't heard the commotion?

"Let him rest," she ordered, wiping her hands on a kitchen towel and then carefully folding it in half and then in quarters. "He's scared to death. I can see it in his face."

I offered her an apology, and then even threw in another one as she left me alone in the kitchen.

"I feel awful," I said loudly, to no one in particular.

At 3:00 p.m. that day, Elise was dressed for her job interview. Jacket, skirt, boots, hair pulled back in a tight bun.

"How do I look?" she said.

"Really sharp."

"Mastic, here I come," she said.

I opened the front door for her and we walked to the Volvo. I was just about to kiss her goodbye and wish her good luck when she went to pieces. I hugged her as her shoulders jiggled up and down, listening to her make a crying sound I had never heard before. It almost sounded like a long, prayerful moan.

"I don't want to work in Mastic," she said, her words muffled against my chest, though I could feel the specific heat behind each one, puffing against my skin.

"Then don't," I said. "Let's just kite checks. Steal his fucking money. Make him pay."

This immediately cut off the moaning and bobbing. She pushed me away, and now in the draining afternoon light, I could see the inky river of mascara pooling around the corners of her eyes.

"What the hell are you talking about?"

"He's evil, Elise," I said. "That's probably why he's not even dying. If he were a nice guy, he probably would have died two months ago."

That was the moment she'd either slap me, defending the bastard, or forgive my outburst.

"I know he's evil," she finally said. "I just thought it was going to be over. We'd get the house."

"It could go on for months. You heard what the doctor said."

Don't bet against him, the doctor had said to us in private, after a quick house call the previous evening. Even without saying a word, Elise and I turned toward each other and knew our hearts were sinking.

"Well, there's no way out," she said, opening the car door and climbing inside. "And maybe there's worse things than being an assistant speech therapist at a speech rehab center in Mastic."

"Sure," I said, trying to look convincing, because at that precise moment I was picturing a room full of moaning adults in an industrial park and Elise cheerily trying to make the best of it with her trusty color-coded flip cards. Pictures of bicycles and mice and flowers. *What vowel do you hear?*

She slammed the door, waved at me, and gunned the accelerator, causing the crows that always sat in the pine tree above the driveway to reluctantly flap away, their surprisingly long wings barely beating at first.

■

As soon as Elise had been gone five minutes, I opened the door to Victor's study, which was directly above his bedroom downstairs. Elise and I, out of curiosity, had already tried to open the safe in the closet, and failed. Short of hiring a professional safecracker, we were left only with Victor's old business correspondence regarding the Hensu Knife. Considering it was a product that no one remembered, it was odd that he had kept photocopies of all the old print ads, and even a satchel full of VHS videotapes containing the knife's thirty-second spots.

I was pawing through the drawer of Victor's desk, searching for anything of value I could give to Carmelita, when I heard the muffled sound of singing downstairs. It was Sandra, cooing Victor his late-afternoon lullaby. I pictured his thin lips peacefully pressed together, his chalky hand squeezing Sandra's fleshy thigh again.

Meanwhile, I was left staring at the magnetic orifice of an old paperclip box. I shook it a couple of times and plucked out one paperclip, unbending it until it was the length of my index finger. Flicking it on the worn carpet, I began to close the drawer when I felt something underneath. In an instant, I was on my knees, tearing off the small manila envelope that he had taped there.

It contained a single brass key that had no marking except for the words SOUTHINGTON, CONN. on the edge. As I listened to Sandra continue her lilting song downstairs, I tore through Victor's closet again, but there was no hidden file cabinet or secret compartment. Just that safe, hidden behind the dry-cleaned jackets he'd probably never wear again.

Eventually, I told myself, I'd find the door or cabinet or shed that key unlocked, but for now I just stuffed it in my pocket and walked downstairs. I was so preoccupied by the key that I didn't even notice Sandra until I got to the bottom step.

She had her coat on and the portable phone was in her hand.

"What's wrong?" I said to her, ashamed that I was secretly hoping that Victor had taken a turn for the worse.

"Crumb cake!" she suddenly shouted at me with a forced smile, her eyes widening. It was like she was speaking to me in code.

"I don't understand," I said, but the words were barely out of my mouth before I heard Victor bark another order from the room.

"Entenmann's!" he shouted.

"My husband is going to pick me up and drive me to the store," Sandra said, keeping her distance from me. "You don't have to worry about a thing."

"Sandra," I said, suddenly hating her for indulging every one of his whims. "You don't have to do this. It's probably the medication talking."

She snorted at that though, actually turned away derisively and waited outside the door for her husband to arrive, glancing through the glass and nervously watching me on the other side. I thought I should open the door and apologize for my loss of control with Victor, but I had the feeling it was a lost cause. Her husband pulled into the driveway a few moments later. He was one of those old-school guys who smoke a pack a day. Forehead as big as a concrete pillbox, and a military crew cut to match. The Buick was filled with trapped smoke and I could hear the strangled sound of some classic-rock song within, though he obediently turned down the radio as soon as Sandra climbed into the passenger seat. I could see Sandra shaking her head as they drove away. She was surely talking about my heartless comment about an ailing man's afternoon wish. I watched the car speed off and then I entered Victor's bedroom.

"I can make them do anything," he said, as soon as I entered the room. "I could get Sandra to kill her husband. It would just take a little patience. You have to put a little thought into it."

"She's getting you crumb cake, Victor," I said. "Don't get too excited."

But he was excited. His slender fingers clenched the top of the sheet that Sandra had lovingly pulled up to his chest, and then he yanked it down. The top of his blue pajamas was soaked with sweat, patches of the cotton turned bluer by the perspiration.

"I could teach you some things," he said softly. "That I've wanted to share for years. But you're just like them. You want to be controlled."

I could have nodded, or laughed, or come up with an insult of my own. But I had no interest in bonding with Victor. Seeing that, he stopped grinning and reached underneath the blanket. Somehow, he had prepared another envelope, though this one was thinner. He held it in his hand, waiting for me to take it.

"Two hundred and three dollars," he said, shaking the envelope in the air as if it were a lure. "It's all I have until Elise drives me to the bank. I want you to give it to Carmelita."

"Only amateurs pay people off in odd numbers, Victor," I said, remembering the tip Elise had playfully given me.

"Who told you that?" he said, a little unnerved. "Carmelita? Tell her I'm getting better. There might be a spring fling, after all."

"I doubt that," I said, taking a seat in the canary-yellow chair that faced him. I noticed it was still warm and wondered if Sandra had sat here while singing, wising up to his searching fingers.

"You know nothing. You heard what the doctor said."

"Cancer is cancer, Victor. It's lighting you up right now, like a pinball machine. You just can't hear all the pinging noises it's making."

He didn't like that. He ran his index finger along the envelope and stared at me, his face darkened as the sun vanished for a moment outside. The light was dimming fast and I was running out of time to visit Carmelita before Elise got back from Mastic.

"Did you find anything in my study?" he said. "I heard your footsteps."

I shook my head slowly, watched him lean forward and adjust a pillow behind his back.

"There's a key there," he said. "Taped under my desk. I'm sure you found it."

"Maybe."

"I locked her up once. I got so worried I'd lose it that I taped it there."

"That's bullshit," I said.

"Is it?" he said, waving the envelope at me tauntingly again. "Why don't you ask her?"

I stood up and faced the window. The scrub pine between the two houses was already turning a washed-out black. In Swain's upstairs bedroom, the lights, still on a timer, popped on. I squinted, but I couldn't make out any figure in Swain's upstairs bedroom.

"You better be on your way," Victor said. "Before Elise gets here. You wouldn't want me to tell her anything behind your back."

I snatched the envelope from his hand, but I didn't leave right away. I got down on one knee, so he could see my face clearly.

"You're a piece of shit," I said softly.

"That's all?" he said, gratified as my face flushed red with impotent anger. I stood up, though every one of my nerve endings wanted to make one decent connection and slap the smirk off his face.

"I'll cover for you, Scott," he said hoarsely, then broke into one of his coughing fits. "I've got your back."

Two hundred and three dollars," Carmelita said, laying the crumpled bills on the coffee table.

"And he's got a message for you," I said, snorting out some disgusted air. "He wants you to stick around until the spring. He says he's feeling better."

Carmelita didn't respond to that. She picked up the money and stuffed it in the pocket of her jeans. It was getting dark in the living room, so I reached for the lamp next to the liquor cabinet.

"Don't do that," she said, walking toward the sliding glass door. I could hear one of the fake leaves from the fake ficus tree crustle under her unlaced boot.

"I won't be able to see you in another ten minutes. We're losing light."

"There's a system with the timer. First the upstairs light turns on, then the one on in the kitchen, then the living room. It's a really comforting routine."

I couldn't entirely make out her expression. Was she joking?

"I have a key," I said, taking it out of my pocket. "I found it under his desk."

"So?"

We weren't making progress as strangers. The simple math was that she didn't trust me.

"He says he locked you up in a closet. Is that true?"

"Maybe," she said.

Since I was standing next to the dusty bottles of liquor, I unscrewed the cap of the bottle of crème de menthe. I took a long swig, realizing suddenly that I'd chosen the Amaretto. The fluid had turned chalky and vile, and I spat it on the floor. Outside the sliding glass door, the sun had finally set, leaving a line of dim red over the hills near the inlet.

She walked toward the kitchen, but I could only make out her silhouette now.

"This is when I usually eat," she said.

"Eat what?"

I twisted the cap on the bottle of Amaretto and touched the other bottles, looking for something with a more familiar shape. I found what looked like a bottle of Tanqueray, and in the dim light, what I thought was greenish glass.

"The things people leave behind," she said. "Cans of stuff. Tins of tunafish. There are other houses." We were standing next to the bare kitchen table. I moved closer to her so I could see her face in the light that was still filtering through the room.

"You break into other places?"

"Only for food. And then there's even a place . . . I don't know if I should tell you this."

The gin, at least, was gin. I took a healthy swallow and felt reassured as it burned all the way down to my lungs. I told her to go ahead, suddenly aware, out of the corner of my eye, that something had skittered across the floor. A mouse? A rat?

"There's one small house on the top of the hill," she said. "An old couple lives there year-round. They sleep like logs when they take their hearing aids out. So once I thought *Why not.* I undressed in their bathroom. I took a hot shower."

I pictured an older couple, wheezing in bed, the unheard sound and unseen steam of Carmelita's shower.

"You can take one at my house," I said. "And you can eat whatever you want."

She laughed at that, finishing with an amused moan.

"Does that turn you on? Allowing me the basic necessities?"

"Of course not," I said. "I'm just trying to be a good guy."

"What would I owe you for a hot shower and some leftovers?"

"Nothing," I said, angry at myself for even having made the offer. Once, when I was photographing a young bride under that tree I'd staked out in Prospect Park, I had told her husband that he was making her self-conscious and had to move farther away. At first the bride had looked concerned as her husband skulked off in his blue tuxedo, eventually sitting on a park bench to anxiously smoke a cigarette. It was a small act of control that made my heart beat faster, as if I'd run two miles. It was the expression on her face that excited me, as she stood there in that cheap gauzy white dress, waiting for me to tell her exactly what to do.

"Hey, good guy," Carmelita said, waving her hand in front of my face. She smiled to let me know she'd let me off the hook for now. "It would never work anyway. Victor told me he'd shoot me point-blank if I ever showed up on his doorstep," she said. "That's the one house I leave alone."

"Why are you scared of him?" I said, taking one more sip of the gin and wiping a warm trickle off my mouth.

"Why are you?"

There was resentment in her voice. It was a bad situation, but she wasn't going to suffer self-righteous questions from a hypocrite. Besides that, it had long since been time to go. I had heard the sound of Elise driving up to Victor's house. The car door slam. Even from within this mausoleum, I was aware of all of that.

"Good night," I said. "I've got to go."

There was this odd formality when I left. Carmelita

always stood up and pulled open the sliding glass door, which was so stippled with rust along its track that it made an alarming racket.

Before I stepped out onto the weedy flagstones, I felt her lips against my cheek. A quick kiss followed by a teasing remark:

"It was a pleasure having you. Do you need a flashlight or can you find your way back?"

"I'm good," I said, reflexively touching the wetness on my cheek, instantly magnified by the colder air outside.

"Can I have the key?" she said. "The one for the closet."

"Why would you want it?"

"One less thing to worry about."

I fished inside my pocket until I found the key.

"Unless you want to lock me up next time?"

She snatched the key from my hand and turned back toward the house before I could tell her that wasn't my thing. I watched her pull the sliding door shut. I could barely see her beyond the darkening blue that reflected off the glass.

Twice, on my way down the gully, I looked back at Swain's home. I thought I could see the top of Carmelita's head, and then her whole body, turned away from me. I supposed she was fixing herself something to eat in the kitchen, or adding Victor's stingy new bribe to some kitchen drawer. All I know is that I fell hard on my knees and elbows, snagged by a tripwire of thorns. When I finally struggled up to my feet, my wrists and face were burning. Climbing over the fence that marked the border of Victor's property, I rolled my sleeve down to cover the fresh scrapes.

When I walked back into Victor's house, it was abnormally quiet. I made my rounds, walking into the empty kitchen and seeing the box of Entenmann's that Sandra had brought. It was sitting in the trash, bent almost in half.

I noticed a half-empty bottle of Shiraz on the wooden table, and a smatter of red drops that Elise hadn't bothered to clean up.

My wife was sitting in the living room, turned toward the dark fireplace. She gave me a strange, detached smile and swirled the wine in her glass.

"How was the interview?" I said.

She patted the chintzy cushion next to her twice, and I sat down.

"I kept on driving," she said.

"Past Mastic?"

"Past Mastic, Shirley, Ronkonkoma. I nearly made it to Queens."

I nodded, trying to stay one step ahead of her as she told me the story of her day. Marital surprises always made me intensely anxious.

"You blew it off."

"Uh-huh," she said, taking another sip of wine. She'd pulled both her legs up against her side, so it looked like she was riding the overstuffed couch sidesaddle.

"That's not good?"

I didn't know what it meant actually. I didn't want to pressure her more by making it a statement.

"There's this incredibly large Gulf station in Centereach. I parked near the air pump and cried like a baby sitting at the bottom of a well."

I tried to put my arm around her shoulder, but she clearly didn't want that. She shrugged off my hand effortlessly, and then she widened her brown eyes and glared at me.

"I fired Sandra," she said. "Just now. The poor woman actually looked devastated."

"Why?" I said. "Was it the crumb cake?"

"He was moaning," she said, allowing a shiver to shake her

shoulders. "I didn't even walk into his room to see what he was making her do."

"Jesus."

"Her husband was out there waiting for her too, smoking his cigarettes in the car. That's my father. His blood turns to sludge unless he's preying on someone."

"Yeah," I said, telling myself that this was the moment to bring up Carmelita. Before another second passed.

"Maybe we should get him an abusive male nurse," I said instead.

That brought a faint smile to her face again, and she ran the palm of her hand along my leg until she reached my knee cap, her fingers curling over.

"Look at me," she said. "I still love you so much sometimes."

The diluted expression of affection chilled me a little, but I let it go. She was having an awful day.

"Glad I could cheer you up."

She took another sip of wine, emptying the glass. She wanted to talk about the Gulf station in Centereach again. For some reason, as I listened to her, I pictured a human-resources manager at an industrial park in Mastic, waiting for her in his cheaply paneled office, her résumé sitting on his polished desk.

"Well, I sat there for a long time, watching strangers walk in and out of the mini-mart. I was trying to figure out who was in worse shape than us. You know, like a family dragging their kid in to pee. Arguing over snacks inside."

"That probably would have been us."

"I'd take it."

I opened my mouth, ready to give her my valedictory speech about weathering the storm, hanging in there, the hope in hopelessness, but all Elise wanted was three things.

"Don't try to cheer me up," she said. "Get me another glass of wine. And see if you can get that fire going."

When I woke up the next morning, I was alone in bed. Elise was fully dressed, standing and watching me. My camera was in her hands.

"What's going on?" I said, turning over on my back.

"What is this?" she said, turning the screen of the camera toward me so that I could see Carmelita's naked, and bruised, breasts.

"I was waiting for the right time to tell you. When you weren't so stressed out."

"What is this?" she said, her voice rising.

"She's a squatter. She lives next door."

"Did you pay this whore to take her clothes off? Did you fuck her?"

I told Elise that the girl wasn't a whore. I swore, of course, that I hadn't touched her. I told her that it was her father who had been bribing her for sexual favors, and that it was her father who had performed these precise acts of mutilation on her body.

"Ask him," I said. "He's the one who told me she was living there. He sent me over there with two envelopes of cash for her."

That settled one thing at least; my wife sailed out of the room with the camera in her hands, and I ran after her in my boxers, wondering what the old prick would say now.

He wasn't asleep. He was watching television his favorite way, with the sound turned down. He couldn't have possibly been interested in the World Series of Poker on ESPN this early in the morning, but he tried to move his head away from the camera as Elise pressed it close to his face.

"Did you hurt this woman?" Elise said. Her voice was more shrill now, and when he tried to avoid looking at the screen again, she grasped his stubbly chin in her hand and tried to force him to see it. He let her hold his face in that position for a moment, and then he sarcastically gasped.

"It's awful," he said. "Who is she?"

"Tell Elise about the winter girl," I said, turning off the television.

"I have no idea what he's talking about," he said calmly to Elise. "Do you?"

"He says you've been giving her cash, Dad. He says she's been squatting next door. What else did you tell him?"

"That was all," he said. "Just an unfortunate I felt sorry for. What else is there?"

"One of you is lying," she said, snorting out a quick laugh. It was as simple as that. She handed me the camera and marched out of the room, grabbing her coat on the way.

"Or all three of us," Victor said to his daughter as she left the room, smiling as widely as he could, despite his depleted energy.

Ignoring him, I turned to follow my wife, running after her until I caught up to her in the driveway, her shoulders hunched forward as she walked onto the road.

"You can't go that way," I said breathlessly. "We've got to walk down to the beach. Walk up those steps to Swain's house."

"You have a system now?" she said, turning toward me again. "You wait till I leave, then scurry off?"

She didn't wait for the answer, and she didn't follow my suggested route either. She cut right through the property that sat on the hill, then downward toward Swain's house. The dry grass we were walking on belonged to an old motel that they hadn't been able to sell for years. But the owner kept it perfectly maintained, even in winter, the sloping lawn cleared of all dead leaves.

Following Elise through some gray branches, one of which snapped wildly and stung my cheek, we emerged on the circular driveway in front of Swain's house, strewn with clusters of dead pine needles.

The door wasn't locked, but at least Elise had the courtesy to knock.

I caught up to her in the living room, where we stood side by side, staring at the decrepit furniture around us.

"Carmelita," I shouted. "I'm here with my wife. She wants to meet you. She wants to hear your story."

Elise glared at me incredulously as I called out the name.

"What's wrong?" I said.

"It just gives me the creeps that you're on a first-name basis already."

"I don't even know her last name. She used to be Swain's housekeeper," I began to explain. "When she came back to see if there was any work, he wasn't here."

But Elise wasn't paying any attention to me, because Carmelita was walking down the curved staircase, wearing the same faded sweatshirt and jeans. I thought for a moment that she might scream at us, or stab at us with some small knife hidden in her pocket, or wolf-whistle for an army of friends who would finally take revenge for what Victor had done. But all she did was sit down on the bottom step, crossing her arms so that her slender fingers anxiously touched each shoulder. We could both see that she was shaking.

"I shiver sometimes," she said, embarrassed. "Not because of the cold. Only when I'm nervous."

Elise took a step toward Carmelita and reached downward, waiting for the woman to shake her hand. It might have taken only a few seconds for Carmelita to acknowledge the gesture, but it felt like much longer. Eventually, she reached up, limply touching Elise's fingers and tugging her hand downward. A strange, mocking handshake.

"Have we met somewhere?" Carmelita said. "Your face looks so familiar."

"No," Elise said. "It doesn't."

Then Carmelita looked at me and had the nerve to raise her thin eyebrows and bite her lip, as if my wife were lying through her teeth.

"My husband showed me some disturbing photographs of some scars on your body," Elise said. "I want to help you."

"Will you call the police?" Carmelita asked, looking at my wife without emotion, waiting for her reaction.

I reached for Elise's hand and squeezed her fingers, surprised at how clammy her skin felt.

"We can do whatever you want. This is serious," Elise said.

"It's very serious," Carmelita said. "But now this wonderful man has sworn to protect me. Do you know how envious I am? Does he make the same promises to you?"

She reached for my free hand and swung it back and forth playfully. I could feel Elise's fingers slipping away from my other hand. She turned around and took a few steps toward the center of the living room, waiting for us to join her. I couldn't remember the last time that Elise's face had such a pained look. I couldn't remember the last time a woman had disrespected her with such subtle accuracy.

"I think we should all sit down," Elise said. "I want to hear your story."

"Whatever you want." Carmelita sighed, swinging my hand one more time through the air and letting it drop away. "But I'm tired of telling stories."

I sat in the ivory-colored chair, wishing I could take another slug of Tanqueray while the two women talked softly on the couch. Elise was holding both of Carmelita's hands and giving her a tremendously earnest look that Carmelita still didn't seem to take seriously. That only made Elise grip the younger woman's fingers tighter as Carmelita calmly explained how her father would sink his teeth into her chest.

I could see that the back of Elise's neck was flushing, and soon the redness had crept into her whole face and her skin glistened.

"But I shouldn't be the only one getting undressed," Carmelita said, reaching for the hem of Elise's T-shirt and starting to pull it up. "Do you have any marks on your body?"

"You're in a state of shock," Elise said, pulling away from her. "You're traumatized and you're going to need help."

I watched my wife turn toward me, give me a funny look, and then she ran toward the sliding glass door and pulled it open. Out on the ruined patio stones, she doubled over and dry-heaved. I went outside and touched her back and told her I loved her, aware that Carmelita was watching us from the living room.

"I don't want to hear the rest," she said hoarsely, gagging again. "She's telling the truth."

I rubbed her back with one hand as she tried to stand up

straight again. She turned and stared at Carmelita, still watching us anxiously from the living room. Not knowing what we were saying, or whether she had something new to fear, she had pulled off her sweatshirt so that we could see her scars.

When I looked back at my wife, her eyes were red and shimmering.

"We kill him," she said softly. "It's the only way we can be happy, Scott. He's going to keep on feeding off our misery as long as he's alive."

"Let's talk about that later," I said, secretly pleased that her rising hatred of her father had forced her to even consider this. But something more immediate was bothering me. "She thinks she knows you. Can you please tell me what's going on?"

Elise turned away from me for a moment and faced the bay. She shielded her eyes for an instant as if she were looking for something threatening on the horizon, or down on the dock below. But there wasn't a single boat in the water, as far as I could see. And no one was watching us from the dock.

"Last summer," she said. "I saw the two of them standing on the beach."

"Where was I?"

"You were back in Brooklyn. You had to shoot some brides in the park."

That was possible. There had been a weekend that Elise had visited her father, but I couldn't even remember which month. It hadn't seemed important to me at the time, and the truth was that we had both been relieved to have the short break from each other. But I did remember that when she returned, she had looked even more stressed out than usual after being around her father.

"I arrived early," she said. "And he wasn't in the house. And then I did what we always do. Go for a long walk. And they were standing on the beach by Swain's house. But we never even shook hands. I just watched her turn and walk the other way."

"And what did he say? Didn't you ask him what he was doing with her?"

"No," she said. "I didn't say a word. I thought he was just flirting with some stranger. I didn't even see her face."

She shielded her eyes again, narrowing them as she scanned the horizon and then lowered her head and stared down at the pier in a peculiar way.

"What are you looking at, Elise?"

"I feel like someone is going to try and hurt us," she said softly, "but I don't know who."

I followed my wife into the gully as she walked away, but she was distracted enough that she tripped over some vines and plunged to the ground.

"Shit," she said, angrily grabbing at my arm and hauling herself up again. She took one look at my face, saw that it was clouded with questions, and kept on walking.

"I believe you, all right?" I said, stepping over a dead pine limb.

"No, you don't, but that's your problem now," she shouted back, her voice echoing in the cluster of curled and twisted pines. It was the most stunted and knock-kneed forest I'd ever seen. A minor hurricane would have ripped all of those fragrant pines out of the shallow graves their roots sat in.

I didn't know how to tell my wife that murdering her father wasn't a good idea, but I couldn't help but feel this twisted sense of relief that she at least saw a future for us. All I knew was that she'd hugged Carmelita and whispered confidential heartfelt things in her ear, and now we were tearing back through the scrub pine and brambles between the two houses.

"Stop," I said, gripping her arm. "Just stop and talk to me."

She pulled her arm away from me, but at least she turned around. She looked so distraught, it was as if she were the one who'd had her breasts bitten by Victor, not Carmelita. Her face was still red and her black bangs clung to her forehead in patches. Through the spindly canopy of pine branches above us, I could see that the sky had turned a dull white again. It looked like it was going to snow.

"She thinks she deserves it," Elise said. "I thought I deserved it. He's got a way of making you feel you're the one that's fucked up inside."

One of her legs gave way, and she grunted softly as I tucked my arm under hers, supporting her. I watched her brown eyes narrow to slits, the ashy breath puffing from her mouth.

"Are you all right?"

"I'm fine," she said. "Just got a little light-headed."

Not far away, I could hear the sound of something that sounded like a Weedwacker. It grew louder until I could see that it was a Cessna, flying toward the inlet, its yellow wings buffeted by the wind. For a moment, I saw us from above, as the pilot would, and wondered what he'd make of us. Why the hell were we stumbling between two houses in the middle of winter? My wife was looking at me imploringly, but my head was still tilted back, watching the small plane until the thin, buzzing sound ceased.

"Why don't we just leave?" I said.

"What if he gets better? Are you comfortable with the idea he'll be over there torturing her while we try to pick up the pieces in Park Slope?"

"The police," I said softly.

"Our fingerprints are all over the house. And who knows

what the girl would say. Do you want to be writing each other sad letters from prison in a year?"

"Elise, you can't even kill a cockroach. You wouldn't even let me buy a glue trap for those mice."

"This is different," she said. "It's his time anyway. Remember? They were saying he would go any day. It was his time, and he weaseled out of it."

That was true, but I still felt the facts were being twisted. The Cessna, which had vanished just a moment before, was circling back. It didn't mean anything, I told myself. Maybe just some pilot on a check flight. But for half a second or so, I wondered how much money Victor had hidden away, and if he had already hired a small team of private detectives to watch every move we made, even from the air. And then there was her brother, our supposed savior, giving criminals the wrong address, but why the house next door?

"How would we accomplish this?" I said. "Ever heard of an autopsy?"

"You think that some coroner is going to get involved? On a weekend in mid-January? For some geezer who's already been given a death sentence by his doctor?"

"I guess not," I said, trailing my thumb up a brown vine studded with thorns. "I have no idea."

"You've got to trust me on this one," Elise said, squeezing my hands. She opened her mouth, her lips perfectly ajar, waiting for a kiss. When I was too slow to offer her one, she leaned in and mashed her lips against mine instead.

We decided that there should be a run-through. First, we'd decided it would be best to be out of the house as Victor drank his laced glass of chocolate-flavored Ensure. Elise would put on her best black cocktail dress, and I would struggle into an old blazer and slacks that I had brought from Brooklyn. They lay waiting for me on the bed, next to Elise's velvet dress. Realizing I had forgotten a pair of dress shoes, I borrowed a pair of Victor's double-tasseled loafers and stared at myself sideways in the mirror as Elise stirred the crushed-up extra-strength Tylenol into his glass. She had just taken a shower, and as she worked on grinding the tablets, the white towel she'd been wearing fell to the floor.

"So when we do this for real," I said, "we use the Percocet."

"Right, right," she said, expertly continuing to stir the glass as she stood there bare naked, the spoon clinking off the sides. "About thirty grams or so, just like this."

"And he won't taste it?"

"Have you ever tasted Ensure? It's vile. He'll never know the difference."

I was looking down at Victor's loafers, and suddenly I felt vaguely sorry for him. He had done his best to preserve the old shoes with a shoe horn, but they looked withered and worn out. You wouldn't be able to give them away at a yard sale.

"Are you ready for our practice run?" she said, turning to face me.

I was looking at the cloudy liquid in the tall glass, and then I found myself staring at the old appendectomy scar on her right side. I don't know how I could have explained it away after seeing the bite marks Victor had left on Carmelita's body. It had the same exact appearance. The purplish scar tissue three inches under my wife's breast fit the shape of her father's teeth exactly, and it looked like a thin, upside-down smile.

"When did he do that to you?" I said.

"It's not important now," she said, pulling open the dresser drawer. She picked out a pair of panties and slipped them on. The silence simply grew between us as she picked out a bra and reached behind her back, hooking it. Then she walked over to the bed, grabbed her dress, and pulled it over her head.

For a moment, she stood with her hands on the dresser, staring at an offending lock of wet black hair in the mirror, and I felt for sure she would finally tell me about the moment her father had sunk his teeth into her flesh, as far as he could, the blood brimming on his stretched upper lip.

"Zip me up," she said. "And get your nice pants on."

All dolled up," Victor said. "What's the occasion?"

He was watching television in the dark, his white face turning bluer or paler depending on the tint of the scene.

"Boredom, I guess," Elise said, placing the glass of Ensure on his bedside table.

"Everybody's got to leave the ranch sometime," I added helpfully, then silently cursed myself. It sounded like code for a homicide, for chrissake. But it didn't seem to faze Elise or Victor, who were now glaring at each other intently.

"Did you talk to Carmelita?" he said, picking up the glass and taking a sip. He didn't seem to detect any difference in the taste.

"Yes," Elise said. "She told us what you did."

There was a milky rim of Ensure on his upper lip now, but he didn't wipe it off.

"What I did?" he said. "Look at me. What could I do to anyone?"

"Plenty," Elise said. "When you could. Do you remember what you did to me?"

Victor seemed to expect this question. He met it with a look of such profound disinterest that I wanted to kill him right then.

"I'm sorry that you think I did something," he said, his voice trailing away. "I seem to remember a young girl who pretended she was having nightmares in order to crawl into my bed."

He glanced at her and had the nerve to actually raise his eyebrows, as if he were expecting an apology.

"Put quite a strain on my marriage, to tell you the truth."

"Because I molested *you*," Elise said softly, watching him take another thoughtful sip.

"You were a very manipulative girl. I'm sure Scott would agree with me if he didn't fear you so much. I don't fear you though. In fact, I think it's time we all stopped pussyfooting around these tiresome sexual issues and get to the really good stuff."

"What's the really good stuff?" I said, horrified. I felt as if I had been jabbed in the solar plexus.

"He'll tell you after we go to dinner," Elise said as evenly as possible. "I'm sure you can spare us until we've had our meal, Dad."

"I'll spare you," he said, uncapping a tube of ChapStick and rubbing it across his lips. "But I'll be wide awake when you get home."

He wanted us to know he had won. He stared at me for some kind of acknowledgment, and then at his daughter, and then at the window and beyond, where the security light in the upstairs bedroom of Swain's house had clicked on again.

"By the way, Scott," Victor said. "Did you give our girl the key?"

"I don't know what you're talking about."

But Elise immediately seemed to know, and when she turned toward me I knew I'd have to answer for that later. For now, she was able to compose herself and devote all of her attention to her dying father.

"Daddy," Elise said evenly, giving him a quick kiss on the forehead that seemed to floor him. "Do you want us to bring you back anything? Some lemon chicken? Some rice?"

"I don't need anything," he said, snapping his gaze away from her and returning it to the television. A German shepherd was being trained to attack an assailant, and it tugged violently at the protective cuff on the arm of its fake victim.

I watched my wife lean closer to him.

"You're going to drop into hell like a stone," she whispered.

These calmly spoken words seemed to take Victor by surprise, but for only an instant. He was an expert at extinguishing any unwanted emotional reaction. But this time, the thin-lipped smile he stretched across his face seemed utterly unconvincing. As Elise moved away he tried to grab her arm, then her hand, but it was too late.

I followed Elise out of the room. We were in the hallway when he called out her name, twice. I stood there, waiting for my wife to come back, but she had already grabbed the car keys. She jangled them once at me, almost teasingly, and walked out the front door.

And same thing tomorrow," I said, sitting in the passenger seat. "Except we really go to dinner."

Elise started the car, placed her hand on the seat rest behind my head, and backed out of the driveway.

"I'm actually starving right now. How about you?"

We drove past the fir with the Christmas lights, which looked as if they were blinking because a cold wind was stirring the branches.

"I liked the last thing you said to him," I said. "You could tell it got to him."

"It's not my line," she said. "My mom told him that just before she died. But he didn't sink anywhere. We just buried her and that was that. But . . ."

"What is it?"

"I think he poisoned her. A day before she ended up in the hospital she'd been feeling fine. And then she was doubled over in pain on a beautiful sunlit lawn. Throwing up while all the children in the neighborhood were laughing and playing."

We were sitting at the intersection of 27 now, and I leaned back so Elise could clearly see the traffic coming in both directions. As usual, being winter, there wasn't a single car in sight. We pulled onto the highway and turned left, toward town.

"Because sometimes I can hear her voice as clearly as his. It's like she never really left."

"You should have told me all of this," I said.

"Before we were married? When we were on that blind date playing pool?"

"Yeah, people do that. They come clean. Secrets burn a hole in everything."

"They were burning a hole in my life before I was even born."

I had to let it go. She was so agitated that she had crossed the median and was in danger of hitting whatever car might come sailing our way.

"You're on the wrong side of the road," I said urgently.

She shook her head, disappointed that this was all I had to say. My own well-being, of course, coming first. Taking her time, she edged back into our lane and then slowed to twenty-five miles an hour.

"Is this safe enough for you?" she said.

I was pushing around the last of my oily fries, looking at the snow falling outside Buckley's Irish Pub. In the nearly empty parking lot, I could see the windshield of our car was already covered with a thin layer.

"Every time I leave his place," Elise said, wiping some teriyaki sauce off her lip, "I feel normal again."

"I don't believe anything that psycho said," I reassured her. "Blaming the victim. You think it's a cliché . . . until it happens right in front of you."

"It's all right," she said, raising her arm for the waitress and forcing a smile. "Down deep I don't even think he knows the truth."

The waitress, a thin woman with a long face and ropy brown hair, coughed in her hand and apologized.

"Don't worry about it," Elise said. "I just want two shots of tequila, lime, and a little salt."

She took our plates and left us alone in the empty dining room. There were two locals at the bar, one staring upward at the television in a forlorn way. The other guy was wearing a red cashmere sweater that had ridden all the way up his back. Even though it wasn't much of a picture, I wished I had my camera.

"We're going to get drunk and drive into a ditch," I said.

"Sounds romantic," Elise said, sliding her hand toward mine.

"You were joking about killing your father," I said softly.

"Why? Did you change your mind?"

I told her I had, which seemed just fine with her. To be honest, I felt intensely relieved. If something could have gone wrong, it would've. The simplest schemes in our lives had never worked out anyway. And there was something else: to that point, other than shoplifting Pop Rocks at a 7-Eleven when I was sixteen, I'd never committed a single crime.

"You gave Carmelita the key," Elise said, having saved this moment to confront me about Victor's revelation. "Why would you do that?"

"It's just a key," I said, leaning toward her so that no one at the bar could hear what I had to say next. "He'd lock her up in the closet for hours. Bleeding, who knows? Scared to death."

"Listen," Elise said, squeezing my hand. "Everything he does before he dies is part of a plan."

"I don't understand."

"That's why we're accelerating the process," she says. "So he can't put all the pieces together and screw us over before he goes."

"It's just a key."

"Does it belong to my dear father?"

"Yes."

"Then it's not just a key. He asked you to give it to her for a reason. And now we'll have to deal with that too."

Elise leaned back in her seat and sighed. She didn't look

entirely miserable either. She looked like she had work to do. Feasible work that might even make her feel good at the end of the day.

The shots were placed on our table. The salt. The slices of lime. Elise propped up my hand with hers and squeezed some juice on it, then shook a thin layer of salt near my thumb. I waited for her to do the same, and then we touched glasses.

"To Victor," she said. "May he rest in peace."

"Or wake up screaming for your forgiveness," I added, knocking back the shot. I wanted another.

"He's not going to wake up."

I'd raised my hand for the waitress again, and when I got her attention I mouthed the words "Two more."

"How's that?" I said to Elise.

"Because there's a very good chance he has ceased to exist. I just wanted to give it an hour or so. I didn't want to hear the dreadful noises."

The old Montauk Highway was a slippery mess, so I didn't exactly drive at breakneck speed on the way back to Victor's. I knew he was dead, because I'd seen how much crushed-up narcotic Elise had dumped into his glass of Ensure. Of course, I'd completely bought her story it was Tylenol and that it was only a dry run.

"This is going to really suck," Elise said tersely. I could smell the tequila on her breath. We'd had another round of shots before leaving Buckley's. Even when we'd stepped out of the pub and walked soundlessly through the snow, nothing felt different. We were still the same old couple, stuck in time.

"You think so?" I said angrily. "Yeah, dealing with a dead body is a pretty big deal."

"Just watch the road."

I did watch the road the rest of the way, and we drove in silence. I turned the wipers to high, but their tiny squeaks couldn't drown out the sound of the tires splashing on the driveway.

We were home. The lights were on in the kitchen, the upstairs bedroom, and Victor's bedroom, just as we had left them.

17

Victor was nowhere to be found.

The television was still on. The sheets had been pulled aside. His black socks were still there beside the bed, crumpled and left next to each other like two dark eyes.

"Dad," I heard Elise call out. It was eerie hearing the lilting tone she used as she called his name into every room, as if she were really concerned about his whereabouts and he might be alive.

"Shoes," I said, picking up one of Victor's special orthopedic sneakers. The other one was lying on its side on the deck. But it wasn't as if he was wearing it. It was as if he had momentarily struggled to put it on, then given up.

If he was in pain, if he were panicking, if he didn't know his daughter had just poisoned him, I knew just where I might find him.

I grabbed a flashlight and ran down to the fence that separated the two houses. It was snowing harder now and I suddenly fell as I pointed the flashlight at the old man leaning against the fence. He had climbed over it and then all his strength had left him.

"Victor," I said, aiming the beam at his narrow white shoulders. His torso was bare, the pajama top balled up in his hand. Moving the beam toward his mouth, I waited anxiously for a frozen breath, but there was nothing.

I climbed the fence, knelt next to him, pointing the flashlight at his face again. One eye had drooped shut. Almost. There was still a watery line of blue and white. The other eye was open, the pupil dime-sized. I waved the light in front of it, still keeping a little distance between the two of us in case he should suddenly reach for my throat. I still believed he was capable of one last, terrible movement, or at least a few words that would change our lives forever again.

"Is he dead?" Elise said.

She was standing about twenty feet away, near the two brown streaks where I had fallen into the snow. When I waved the flashlight at her face, she looked petrified, as if she had expected him to die with his hands neatly crossed in bed and a note thanking her for his last drink.

"Yeah," I said, turning off the flashlight, because I didn't want to see anything for a few seconds. I wanted to gather my thoughts before I thumbed it on again. Across from us the timer in Swain's house was flipping switches again. The upstairs bedroom light went dark, but not before I had time to see Carmelita standing there, leaning against a wall as if she had been waiting for us for a long time. Downstairs, the kitchen lamp came on, throwing its slanted square of light all the way to the edge of Swain's patio.

I was the one who grasped Victor's cold fingers and dragged him back to the bottom of the deck. Once, I paused because I thought I heard him exhale. I waited there, the flashlight aimed at his head by his daughter. The snow, still falling, had begun to cover the deep-set wrinkles in his face.

I knew I was going to have to carry him over my back in order to get him up the stairs. Elise waved the flashlight at the bottom step as I wrapped my arms around him and pushed him up, until I could feel his chin fall heavily on my shoulder. Even in the cold, I could feel a semi-warm thread of saliva, or blood, ooze from his mouth and spread over my shoulder.

"Did you see her?" Elise said.

"Who?" I said, breathless, moving toward the bottom step as Victor and his silken pajama bottoms began to slide out of my arms.

"Carmelita," she said. "She was watching us."

"Can you help me?" I shouted back. "This is a fairly new concept for me."

She waved the flashlight at the third, then fourth step. It occurred to me, as I hugged Victor tighter, that he had an unmistakable hard-on. I'd read about this happening to hanged men, but now his prick was pressed against my stomach. One last, perverse joke. Even though he'd never get to enjoy it.

At the top of the deck, I laid him down, the back of his head thunking rudely against the all-weather planks. Elise turned off the flashlight and stood over her father, watching the snowflakes catch on his chin and the hairs of his chest. His pajama top was balled up in her hand.

"Can you prop him up?" she said.

I dug my hands under his armpits and made him sit up, and she raised one of his arms, tugging the sleeve up to his elbow, and the shoulder. I tilted him forward and she pulled back his other elbow, found his fingers, and dressed him for the last time.

Three buttons were missing, surely covered by a fresh inch of snow. The pajama top fell open all the way to his waist.

"It'll have to do," she said, standing up again. She turned and faced Swain's house again, looking at it uneasily.

"What's wrong?"

"She's watching everything. I know she's standing there right now."

"She's probably happier than you are," I said, pulling open the screen door. I used my foot to keep it open, then dragged Victor into his own living room. I let his hands fall to the floor, and then I raised mine to my face, wiping some snot off my nose. My hands smelled like the lavender lotion Sandra had massaged into his knuckles every day. Turning away, I stared at the brass statuette of a rodeo rider on the mantelpiece until the lurching feeling in the pit of my stomach passed.

When I looked back at Elise, she had covered her mouth and looked away too, her shoulders rhythmically moving up and down, the same way they had before she left for Mastic.

"I can't believe you let me talk you into this," she said, glaring at me, her fingers still pressed against her runny nose.

I wouldn't say it was a revelation, just a small moment of dread that might have passed for one. Why should it surprise me that she'd turn it around and blame anyone but herself? It was in her blood. The complete set of genes responsible, lying on its back on the floor.

"You can get it from here?" I said tersely. "I'm going upstairs to take a shower. I've got to wash your father off me."

I smelled like coughed-up Ensure, lavender blossoms, and the vaguely corked smell of dried blood. It was blood, after all, that had spilled from his mouth.

"Just change your clothes," Elise said. "We don't want to look too nice when the ambulance people get here."

18

214 Windmill Lane.

A quaint little Cape Codder near the railway tracks and the water tower in Southampton. And the day outside, brilliantly blue and frigid.

Elise and I sat across a long conference table from David Read, Victor's lawyer. I had expected some gruff, potbellied local who wore a suit and tie even in the depths of January. But what we got instead was someone fresh out of law school, wearing a comfy North Face vest and tearaway track pants. He looked like one of those pleasant, oval-faced jocks you see walking with their sharkish-looking girlfriends on the Upper East Side on a Sunday morning. He had been working out at Omni Fitness, he said, when we had called him.

Just like Victor, I thought, to pick the most junior guy at the firm to save a few bucks. God knows what pennies were in store for us. In the car on the way over, Elise and I had placed bets on what he would leave us. I wagered he would leave us some contemptuous appliance, like the backup microwave he had refused to throw out when he purchased its replacement. Elise was certain he wouldn't even leave us that. It didn't matter to her, she said. She was going to fight it in court. She'd read about other children who'd at least managed to rescue a small portion of a deceased parent's property.

"Here it is," David Read said, plucking a long blue folder from a pile of other folders. "Just give me a minute."

Elise laid her hand on the conference table, and I reached over to squeeze it. Even after taking four compulsive showers and soaping myself relentlessly, I still felt like I could detect that lavender scent. I knew it was my mind playing a trick on me, but in the end, what's the difference?

"Nearly there, nearly there," David Read said, wetting his thumb on a blue circular sponge and flicking another page upward. "Here we go. No, that's not it."

I looked out the window again, focusing intensely on a rusted patch on the railway bridge. I thought I might be sick again, especially if I let my mind wander back to the sound of the stretcher being un-collapsed inside the house. The sleepy voice of a dispatcher on a bulky walkie-talkie, in a town that had no other emergencies. We told them exactly what had happened. We went to dinner. We came back. He wasn't breathing.

Despite this information, the younger paramedic got out his portable defibrillator and tried to shock Victor back to life three times. And I really thought we were done for. That it would work and his dried-out, open eyes would blink, and it would all start over again. I told the paramedic that Victor got a little loopy when he took his nightly meds and had wandered outside while we were having dinner. As he waved a pen light in front of Victor's fixed pupils, I told him we had found him half naked in the snow. The grit and dead pine needles stuck to Victor's skin must have made my story seem believable, because he only murmured something about late-stage hypothermia and "paradoxical undressing." Elise and I solemnly followed the stretcher as it noisily rolled over the carpet. They slammed the doors of the ambulance, the red and blue of its emergency lights exploding harmlessly in the pine trees around us.

"So," David Read said, "if you'll give me a minute here while I read this over."

We gave him a minute, watching his lips move as he read the words. He looked up with a pleasant smile and told us it was a fairly straightforward last will. Victor had left Elise everything.

Our day chugged ahead as if it had been planned by someone else. At 10:00 a.m., we'd found out that Elise had inherited Victor's house, Swain's house and property, and 297,300 shares of the Hensu Knife Company, which in turn was bought by the Scott Fetzer Company, and in turn Berkshire Hathaway. After picking up Victor's neatly boxed ashes at the O'Connell Funeral Home on Little Plains Road, a quick call to an investment adviser at Hathaway confirmed that the shares were worth approximately $2.8 million.

"I'm feeling guilty about not spending a little extra for a coffin," Elise said, as I drove down Hill Street toward Victor's house. Yesterday's snowstorm had almost melted away, leaving only a few traces of itself on the wigwam outside Navajo Joe's Trading Post.

"I think once you murder somebody, you really shouldn't worry too much about the small things."

She laughed at that, and I tried to. Victor, even tucked away in heavy plastic in that featureless cardboard box, offered us no particular advice.

"Who knows how many times he changed his will," she said, staring out at the thicket of branches as we veered onto Westway. There was a FOR SALE sign on the first property in the cul-de-sac, a timber-framed ranch home that blended in drearily with the forest behind it. We could afford that one now, and two or three more. Another spasm of nervous excitement took hold of me. I couldn't stop imagining certain financial possibilities. A black Lexus passed us as we drove toward the bay and I glanced at it, imagining the smell of leather and a warmed, pre-reclined seat.

I could build a darkroom somewhere. I could afford a bottle of Pappy Van Winkle on eBay.

"He didn't change his will though," I said, parking the car at the boat ramp at the end of the road, just a few yards from the water. It was still and light blue. The color of her late father's eyes.

"He had an appointment with his lawyer. He would have found a way to fuck us over before he died."

To tell you the truth, Elise looked a little abject. Even though the heat was blasting in the car, she was hidden deep inside her gray parka, the hood pulled up. She reached back for her father's container, generously adorned with a plastic handle, and walked down to the edge of the water. I left the keys in the ignition and joined her there.

"I don't know how to do this," she said, looking down at the box. "Maybe there's a better place."

I didn't say a word. I just took it from her, and she gratefully stood back as I ripped off the handle, then tore open the flaps and pulled out the heap of ashes in the thick plastic bag. They looked more like what's left in a fireplace than something fine and powdery, with visible pieces of bone and something that looked a lot like the brass button of the cardigan he'd been dressed in for the final viewing. No one had attended.

To our left, an aging golden retriever appeared, wagging its whole hind end happily as it greeted us.

"Sammy," its cheerful owner shouted. "Leave those people alone."

He called the dog's name again, his beaming expression fading as he noticed the plastic bag in my hands. Pulling the dog away by the collar, he continued walking, not letting go of Sammy until he was another hundred yards away.

"Let's get this over with," I said, kicking off my sneakers and then pulling off my socks.

"I'll come with you," Elise said, doing the same. "I'm not just going to stand and watch you from the shore."

Pants rolled up to our knees, we waded into the freezing water, wincing as our feet touched down on broken clamshells and sharp pebbles. In the distance, visible only as a dot of brown, barely distinguishable from the sand, Sammy was still obsessed with us, his hoarse barking carrying along the surface of the water. I peeled off the thick clasp tie and opened the bag.

"Is there anything you want to say?"

"I don't feel like it's real yet," Elise said, keeping her eyes on the shimmering inlet, where a beacon blinked on and off, even at midday. She shaded her eyes so that I could see only the smile breaking across her face. "How about you?"

"I'm working on it," I said, that nervous excitement caught like a ball of rubber bands in my throat. I let the ashes pour out of the bag. The residue simply floated around us. The only thing that sank was that fucking brass button, and even that I could still see, nine inches underneath the water, already nipped at by a pinkie-sized fish.

In silence, we walked back to our sneakers and socks and shoes, gently stooping down to unroll our pants over our wet skin.

■

What do we do about the girl?" Elise said. She was sitting at the kitchen table, scrawling circles inside of circles and then decorating them with crosshatches. We were waiting for her bank officer to call her back, letting us know whether Victor's Hensu shares had been transferred in kind to Elise's Chase account.

"She probably took off," I said. "And who cares anyway? She doesn't have any idea what happened."

"She sees Victor lying dead against the fence. She sees us dragging him back into the house."

"So he goes nuts at the end. You think he's the first old guy who dies wandering around in the snow?"

Continuing her frenzied doodling, Elise pushed the pen deep into the notepad, giving the crosshatches each a rectangle, and then the rectangles each shot off a pointy arrow. The phone rang and she instantly stopped.

"Yes, this is she," my wife said.

She didn't even notice that I had stood up and put on my jacket. I grabbed the Nikon on the counter and started to tell her where I was headed. I watched her cover the phone with her hand, biting her lip hard as another girlish smile broke across her face.

"I love you," she said, quickly unclasping her hand and turning her attention back to the conversation. "So it's in the account, but it's not technically there yet? I think you're going to have to explain that to me."

Carmelita saw right through me. I even felt embarrassed that I'd tried to invent a stupid story.

I was sitting on the couch in Swain's house, listening to the echoes of my increasingly high-pitched voice bounce off the walls. She was sitting in the fake ivory chair, her knees drawn up to her chest, her arms clasped around her legs.

"You don't believe me," I said, not even bothering to tell her the rest.

"Not a word."

"Well, it's true."

I watched her, I must admit, a little tensely, as she stood up and walked over to me.

"I was sleeping," she said, "and I thought I heard Victor calling my name. But very faint."

Carmelita sat down next to me, her leg touching mine. I frowned prudishly and moved away from her.

"I can hear you fine from there," I said.

This amused her so much that she pinched the bridge of her nose and shook her head sadly, as if she was trying very hard not to laugh in my face.

"I put my jacket on," she said. "I walk down there until I see him. He tells me that the two of you have tried to kill him. Very raspy voice. Can hardly hear him at all."

"He was a very paranoid guy, Carmelita. He thought his own doctor was trying to finish him off."

"I get very close to him," she said, ignoring me, "so I can hear what he is trying to say. He wants my help. That is all he wants. *Help me, help me, help me.* I knelt there until I couldn't hear those words anymore."

"So we're all involved," I blurted out, turning toward her angrily. "You did the right thing. You didn't lift a finger. You didn't call the police."

"Give me your hand," she said, holding her palm upward.

"Why?"

"I'll tell you in a second."

I gave her my limp fingers, expecting her to turn them

over and trace some strange fortune. Instead she stood up, tugging at me gently.

"What are you doing?" I said.

"You're going to follow me."

I walked a step behind her, my hand still in hers as she guided me into the kitchen and turned on a flimsy overhead fluorescent light. We walked down the narrow plywood stairs. It was just at the bottom that I pulled away, watching her turn on another light in the dank room.

It was like any basement anywhere: concrete walls, casement windows that were caked with sea salt and dust. There was some garden equipment rudely jumbled in a corner. Rakes and bags of rock salt and sacks of mulch and a lawnmower still scabbed with a summer's worth of dry grass. The rest of the floor was bare except for the floodlight that showed the fine layer of dust on an old washer and dryer in the other corner. Flaps of gray lint filled a small galvanized bucket next to it.

She took my hand again and led me toward the washer. A plastic bucket was filled with freshly washed clothes.

"Still works," she said, drumming her nails on the top of the washer. "Just cold water though. Anything you need washed?"

"I'm good right now," I said as she unzipped her sweatshirt. The fluorescent light above us was faintly buzzing.

I watched her open the washer door and throw it in. Then she unsnapped her jeans and stepped out of them, her eyes locked on me the whole time. She tossed those in the washer too, then her socks, and a pink T-shirt. Staring at me without a hint of self-consciousness, she reached behind her back and unsnapped her bra, throwing it into the basin too. That left me fully dressed next to a woman I still barely knew, wearing only a faded pair of blue panties. She cranked up the dial of the washing machine as if she were setting a timer and folded her arms over her small breasts. The ever-present chill in the house pinpricking her light brown skin with goose pimples again.

I heard a creaking noise upstairs and froze.

"Don't worry so much. It's only the wind. The house does what it wants," she said, quickly touching my neck and then letting her hands fall to my waist. She pulled me closer so that we were leaning on the washing machine. But when she tried to kiss me I pulled away. I couldn't stop picturing Elise. What if she was standing right above us? What if she was just feet away from the open basement door?

"The door's open," I said.

"So close it," she said, unscrewing the top of a bottle of detergent and pouring a thin stream of the blue liquid on top of her crumpled clothes. I left her there for a moment and climbed back up to the top of the basement stairs. And then I said goodbye, I'll see you soon, I've got to get back to Victor's house, to my wife, to my marriage.

I really did say all those things in my head, as I stood on the second-to-last step and stared into the kitchen and beyond at the flashing light on the bay. There were some fishing boats clustered near the inlet, so far off they could have been a gathering of gnats, suspended in the cold white. Then I closed the door, softly, I might add, and walked back down the basement steps.

Carmelita's hands were on the drier and her legs were spread outward. More muscular than I thought they'd be for a squatter who sat in a chilly living room all day. She turned her head playfully to me as I walked down the last steps.

"I want you to stop right there," she said, arching her spine a little. "And think what's it going to be like to grab my ass."

"I'm thinking," I said, taking another step.

"Don't move," she said, suddenly angry. "I hate when people can't stick to the rules. When you stick to the rules you can do anything."

It felt like she'd learned that from someone. It sounded like Victor, one hundred percent.

"All right," I said, closing my eyes for a moment, imagining my fingers digging deep into her ass, pulling her buttocks apart to get a better look. When I opened my eyes I could see that she was enjoying my frozen state. Underneath the thin strip of her blue panties, I could see that her pussy was glistening.

"Take my panties off," she said.

"In my head?" I said uncertainly, not wanting to screw this up. "Or for real?"

"For real, you clown."

I only grazed the small of her back at first with my fingers, and she moaned very softly, more like a vibration I could feel all the way down her spine. I began to peel back her panties and pulled them down her legs. I was kneeling as she quickly stepped out of them. I stood up again, lifted up the lid of the washer, and the water, already coursing into the basin, stopped. I dropped the panties and closed it again.

"Hurry up and fuck me," she said, "before I get cold."

I wanted to get it over with as fast as possible. I'll say that for myself. As if it were some kind of rule of infidelity—if I kept it short, my marriage stayed alive. But just allowing myself to touch her narrow waist for a few seconds turned into just allowing myself to enter her for a few seconds, and then fucking her harder than I'd ever fucked Elise. Who, by the way, was screaming my name, asking where the hell I was. I could hear her muffled voice through the casement window.

"Wait," she said, sliding off my cock before I came. She squatted before me and pushed her small breasts together, the black bite marks still visible, outlined with a vile line of purplish red, as if the puncture would never heal. In the flat white fluorescent light, I could see other places where Victor had gnawed at her. Two raised and still reddened C's near her leg, like two smiles facing each other. And then I pictured him opening his mouth that wide, as wide in my mind as a snake dislocating its jaw to feed on some small animal. His saliva streaking her skin.

I felt my breath get shorter and shorter as I tugged away.

"I want you to do terrible things to me," she said. "Worse than he ever did. Promise me."

I nodded, but that wasn't enough.

"Say it," she shouted at me. "Tell me you want to keep me trapped here like an animal. Torture me."

"I promise," I said, watching her pinch her dark nipples and tug them upward, the dark scar tissue under her breasts gleaming in the sunlight.

"Tell me I'm a cunt and you're going to fuck me up," she said.

"I'm going to fuck you up, cunt. You're not going to look the same after I'm done with you. I'll tie you up and break your bones right in front of you."

"That's better," she said. "Maybe one day when you're ready I'll give you the key."

She looked up at me, unblinking, as my sperm began to land on her breasts and neck and lips.

"I'm going to fucking flay you," I said.

"You promise?" she said. "You can do better than a sick old man."

She seemed to gleefully ignore the increasingly panicked sound of my wife yelling my name.

"You're taking pictures in your mind," Carmelita said. "I can see it in your eyes."

■

You're not in love anymore," Carmelita said, wiping my come off her chest with a paper towel. "Is there any on my neck?"

She lifted up her chin playfully and I nodded gravely. I'd become her human shame mirror.

"Yeah," I said, looking back down at the concrete floor as I tugged my pants back on. I was listening to the wet slosh of the washing machine. In the cold air, my sweat had dried instantly.

I told her I had to go and squinted up at the light at the top of the basement stairs. For the first time, I noticed the moisture seeping through the walls, the threadlike legs of a daddy longlegs paused on the pockmarked Sheetrock behind us.

"Sometimes things change so fast you don't even feel it," she said. She finished wiping my come off her chest and then crumpled up the paper towel and tossed it in the lint bucket. "By the time your brain catches up, it's too late."

I was thinking about evidence now. How much I was always leaving behind in the house. Fingerprints, footprints, and now a soiled paper towel sitting in a galvanized lint bucket.

Elise was calling my name again, but her tone had changed. It was accusing now. She wasn't excited to tell me that everything was okay with the bank; she was homing in on me. Glancing out of the casement window, I could see her legs moving toward the edge of Victor's property.

"I'll give you some money," I said. "But you have to leave us alone."

"Five hundred and six dollars?" Carmelita said, tucking a few strands of hair behind my ear and then gently tracing a long vein on the side of my neck with her finger. "Maybe six hundred and eleven?"

"It'll all be nice even numbers from now on," I said, trying to head off her sarcasm. "Bigger amounts."

"Scott!" Elise screamed. She must have been on the pool deck now, because I could hear her voice echoing off the wood. The tone of her voice had changed one more time. There was more worry in it now, as if something bad might have happened to me. Or maybe something even worse: that I was conspiring with this girl against her.

As my wife continued to make her way toward me, Carmelita leaned over and pulled a fresh blue T-shirt from the plastic bucket and pulled it on, then a new pair of striped panties. Finally, a fresh pair of jeans that were a size too big for her.

"I wear anything I find around here," she said, for the first time a little self-conscious. Anything that touched on money or material almost made her look like her soul was caving in. There was another sweatshirt in the bin, an old gray Champion that Dick Swain must have once worn. She pulled that on too and then she asked me if I liked secrets.

"I know something about your wife that you don't," Carmelita said.

"Let's not get too mystical here," I said, turning away from her and watching the daddy longlegs scurry back up to a crevice near the ceiling, where the sorry thing was still completely visible.

"She's a born thief."

"How would you know?" I said, angry now.

"Because Victor told me. He says it used to be a real problem. She'd take anything she thought she could get her hands on. It took a while for her friends to catch on, but pretty soon no one wanted to invite her over anymore."

I thought my wife must be standing right outside the sliding glass door now, cupping her hands and peering through the plastic covering the shattered glass. Why didn't I hear the muffled sound of her calling my name again?

"So what?"

"It's not a big deal. But just one of a hundred things I could tell you about her."

"Victor's a born liar," I said. "He was manipulating you, Carmelita."

Walking to the door, I could hear the pathetic sound of Elise lightly tapping her knuckles against the intact glass.

"What's another thing?" I said, wishing I hadn't asked that question about my wife as soon as it came out of my mouth. Carmelita seemed to relish my moment of insecurity. She moved closer to me and tried to kiss me on the mouth, but I turned away.

"How about I tell you one secret a day?" Carmelita said, running two slender fingers down my chest. "That'll make you too scared to even go home."

"I'm not as gullible as I look," I said, but the truth was I was starting to believe everything.

"She used to have a half sister," Carmelita said. "Two years younger than her. The girl followed her around like a puppy."

Elise was calling my name again, but it was farther away. I imagined she must be exploring the weedy edges of Swain's property now, or carefully treading down the ruined stairs that led to the pier.

"What happened to the half sister?" I said, impatient now. I didn't want to just stand there facing her, looking confused. Elise and I had major problems, but we still weren't finished. I reminded myself I was listening to a squatter who had allowed herself to be tortured by Victor for a few hundred dollars. Maybe this was just another way of getting paid.

"I don't know," Carmelita says. "Victor says she just disappeared. But then out of nowhere, one day, she calls him again."

"I'll double-check that with my wife."

"I don't know if you should double-check anything with her. Victor told me Elise was the one I should fear the most. He told me that after he was through with his biting once. I was crying. Maybe I looked like I'd call the police."

"I'm going to tell her you're gone," I said, walking toward the stairs. "I'll bring you the money later tonight, and then it's over."

"Scott," Carmelita said, pinching her nose and wincing, as if she were trying to recall something.

"What is it?"

"I want to show you something."

"My wife's ten feet away. She's looking for me."

But she wasn't anymore. There was no more shouting of my name. Maybe she was scrambling down the gully now, or the stairs; maybe she was shading her eyes at the end of the dock, wondering if I'd drowned myself.

Carmelita confidently took my hand and led me to the other side of the stairs. The brass key I'd given her was sitting in the keyhole of a closet door.

"Open it," she said.

The contraption was a very narrow *L*-shaped wooden chair nailed to the floor. It was this closet that the brass key unlocked. There was a circular band of black nylon that was attached to the back of the chair and two more bands around the armrests.

"What is it?" I said.

"Sit in it," Carmelita said.

"Are you crazy?"

"Then I will."

She squeezed past me and sat in the small chair.

"He fastened the Velcro straps," she said. "I know it's only Velcro, but you can't move an inch."

"Then what?"

"He locked the door. See the lightbulb? It's on a timer, like all the rest of the lights, but it only stays on for half an hour. That's how you know one day has gone by, or two, or three."

"He kept you here for three days?"

"Six days once. I was so weak afterward he had to carry me out in his arms like a child. He liked that the most. He used to tell me it's the sweetest part of being a father. The helplessness of the child."

"Well," I said, my anger an acidic burn in my throat. "Why don't we try for seven days? How about fourteen?"

"Listen, Scott," she said softly. "You can't just invade a woman's life and leave her worse off. It's not good for anybody."

I heard Elise's voice again, closer now. But she wasn't calling my name, she was urgently talking to someone on her cell phone. I made out only a few phrases, but I distinctly heard *You're going to have to get your ass down here.* Elise must not have been satisfied with the response she got on the other end, because whoever it was she was talking to had hung up. So she called back again. *Answer your phone,* she hissed.

"What do you call that silly knife that used to be on TV?" Carmelita said. "They'd give you an extra one for free to chop tomatoes."

Elise, unable to work up the nerve to enter Swain's home by herself, was now knocking on the sliding glass door of the living room again. This time, a little more insistently.

"I have no idea," I said, walking up the basement stairs.

Carmelita stayed where she was, and when I glanced back at her, she made a quick chopping motion with her right hand.

Of course, Victor had told her about his $2.8 million. Hung it over her head so that she'd do the little things he needed.

"Walk up the stairs faster," Carmelita said, giving me advice as I ascended the steps and caught sight of Elise cupping her hands and peering inside. "You've just heard her knocking. You were exploring the empty basement. You found nothing. And zip up your pants, Captain."

I did just as I was told, which seemed to delight Carmelita. I could still hear her gently laughing as I closed the basement door behind me.

Elise saw me at the last moment and lurched back, turning toward the sea, as if she might run all the way down the hill.

I pulled open the sliding door and joined her on the patio.

"She's gone," I said, glancing back at the house. "No sign of her anywhere and I've been in every room."

"Did you hear me calling you?"

"I was in the basement. You have no idea how much junk I had to wade through down there."

I was explaining the many potential hiding spots in the dank basement when Elise flung her arms around my neck, pulling my head down until my forehead touched hers.

"I thought I was going to get sick," she said. "You don't even know how fast my heart was beating. I thought she had killed you. I thought I'd find you lying on the floor in there somewhere."

I kissed her on the lips, quickly, because I thought she

might somehow smell Carmelita on my skin. Then I squeezed her hand and started to lead her away from the house, but she wouldn't budge.

"I thought I just heard someone call my name," she said anxiously. "Did you just hear that? Like sort of mockingly?"

"No," I said, using a little more force to drag her away from Swain's home. "Believe me. You didn't hear anything."

Elise had found an ancient cigarette she had tucked away in a small velvet-lined box on the sideboy, and we shared it on the deck. We stooped forward, passing the Marlboro Red like a joint, exhaling through our teeth. The temperature had dropped below freezing again, but it was still early in the day.

I handed Elise what remained of the cigarette and we both turned toward Swain's house. I breathed a little more easily when I saw that Carmelita was not standing and watching us from the window.

"I heard her voice," Elise said, crushing out the cigarette against the railing. A few sparks flared away, and she flicked it into the dark.

"There was no one there," I said, staring across the gully.

"Where is she?"

"I told you I searched the whole house. Why would I lie to you?"

"I don't know, Scott. We're not getting along. You just watched me poison my father. Maybe you're hedging your bets."

Little thief, I was thinking, picturing her as a young girl, stealing money from the wallets of guests who had come for dinner. *Little murderer.* What had happened to her half sister? What were the other ninety-eight secrets Carmelita had promised?

"I'm telling you," I said. "I searched everywhere. The basement. The closets."

"You fucked her."

"Elise."

There's something I always do when I'm lying and I need time to think. I repeat the first name of the person I'm lying to. It's just one of the reasons I'm a terrible liar.

"Just tell me the truth. Get it over with."

I listened to myself tell her the truth, chipping away at any unnecessary detail. It had been quick and disgusting. I felt fucking terrible. I was a stressed-out mess. I wasn't thinking right.

"I'm a mess," I said again. "I'm so sorry."

I waited for her to scream at me or slap my face, but she did nothing. When she opened her mouth, her frozen breath curled toward me and vanished, curled toward me again.

"It's freezing," she finally said in a voice that sounded much too calm. "Let's go inside."

I opened the door and followed her in. On the dining room table she had spread out all of Victor's old papers. Heaps of correspondence that she had started to separate into distinct piles before seemingly losing interest. There was a single Christmas card, looking very regal in a large red envelope, Victor's name ornately handwritten on the front. I tucked my index finger underneath the flap and tore it open.

It was a photo of Richard and Martha Swain, sitting in two large armchairs and tilted lovingly toward each other. Her white hair is cut short, but she looks remarkably healthy. It's Dick Swain who's gained weight, his face a sunburned red. On a table in front separating them were two porcelain statues of Mr. and Mrs. Claus, about the same height as the porcelain pig.

On the back was written:

Merry Xmas from the Capri Rehab (skilled nursing, Victor! Martha says this is the place for you!). Here's to visiting the real Capri next summer and swimming in the Blue Grotto. Thanks for watching over the house. I know it's been an eternity. We shall return!
Yours R&M.

"Who's it from?" Elise said.

"The Swains," I said, stretching out my hand so she could see it. "Apparently, they're alive and well in Phoenix."

She took the card from me and silently read it, then neatly ripped it up in four exact quarters and tossed it into the fireplace.

"So much for your blackmail idea," she said.

"Whose blood is on the bed, then?" I asked her. I felt my back muscles getting rigid, the pain spreading outward toward my shoulders. I saw myself tearing off the comforter, and I saw the shape of that bloodstain again, turned yellow at its farthest edges.

"How do I know?" Elise said. "You think I'm one step ahead of you? Finding ways to make this even more terrible?"

"All right, all right," I said, looking at what remained of the convalescing Swains in the fireplace. Were their bags packed? Were they on their way back? Would we have to kill them if they started to find evidence in their own house? The house that Victor had bought from them. Did they think they'd get it back somehow? Was Carmelita staying put because she thought it had been promised to her? One last sadistic empty gesture.

"They'll be there for months," Elise said, crouching near the fire and striking a match. The remains of the Christmas photo turned black as they caught fire. "She still looks like death warmed over."

■

How about a drink?" Elise said, glancing at me over her shoulder as she walked toward the kitchen. "There must be a bottle of something left."

"Sounds good," I said morosely, sitting down on one of the dining room chairs and picking up a single flimsy yellow invoice from the stack. It was for one pair of Magnanni Medallion-Toe Oxfords, two hundred and ninety-five dollars.

"Why don't you make sure that fire doesn't go out?" Elise said from the kitchen. "And we'll get drunk on whatever's left."

I had pretty much polished off whatever was left, including the last of the Cutty Sark. But Elise announced that she had found a bottle of old Cognac deep in the cabinet.

"I think it's VSOP," she said. "The label's kind of ripped off."

"How about one of those skunky beers in the back of the fridge?" I said, unable to prevent myself from picturing the spiked Ensure she had handed Victor.

I heard the clunky rush of ice cubes spilling from the dispenser, then one skittering across the floor. I put my hands on my knees, stood up, walked to the fire, and did as I was told. There was a stack of fresh newspapers that Victor had tried to read the week before. Sandra adding each *New York Times* and *Wall Street Journal* to the stack on the right of the fireplace. I tore off a sheet of Thursday's *Journal* and crumpled it up, adding it to the two logs that were already sitting on the andirons.

I was reaching for the box of safety matches when I heard the ice clinking in the glass behind me. I listened to Elise set it down on the dining room table, and then I heard the distinct metallic snap.

When I turned around, I had just enough time to see her

tuck the second red shotgun shell into Victor's old Browning, and then she snapped the gun shut and aimed it at the general vicinity of my chest.

I was already crouched by the fire, which was a fortunate thing, because I suddenly felt so light-headed I thought I was going to pass out. I wanted to say something important to Elise that would change her mind, but the back of my tongue felt as if it had doubled in size. I couldn't speak.

"This is the one thing Victor left you in his will. Isn't that funny?" she finally said.

I nodded. I thought it was vital that I laugh, but all I could manage was two small coughs. Elise took another two steps toward me, close enough now that she could safely aim the gun at my skull and be sure she would blow off the top of my head.

I love you, I wanted to say. Or *Holy shit.* Or *Please don't.* But all that came out of my tongue-trapped throat was another boyish cough. On the verge of bursting into oblivion, it was as if I was becoming younger and younger. And then that familiar shaking began. My legs, my arms quivering. Then my whole jaw doing the sewing-machine bit. My eyes welling up. I didn't want to stare at her finger, my wife's slender familiar index finger curled around the trigger, so I bowed my head. On my knees, I bowed my head, and I waited.

"Scott," she said. "What the fuck are you doing?"

When I looked up at her again, she had taken another step to my left and now she was carefully resting the gun against the wall. She took the box of matches from my hand, knelt next to me, and struck one, holding it to the edge of the newspaper until it caught fire. I could suddenly feel the spit in my mouth again.

"I thought," I said to her softly, "that you were going to shoot me."

I waited for her to answer me and provide some kind of clarification, but she just leaned back and sat on the carpet, watching the flames spread.

"I need to know everything that woman said to you," she said.

I sat down on the couch and softly punched one of the flowery pillows near the armrest. Once, when we had first arrived here after Victor's hospitalization, I had gotten a little drunk and spilled wine all over the couch. I thought it was a tragedy until I realized Victor had Scotchgarded the whole thing. It wiped off as easily as water. Which was more than could be said about the blood on the bed next door.

Elise poked at the fire a little more and then sat down in the armchair across from me.

"She says she's got a hundred secrets about you, Elise," I said. My voice sounded hoarse, and I lamely punched the pillow again. Elise had changed position and had crossed her legs. Her face framed by the *L* of her fingers. She seemed to be sizing me up like one of her speech patients. One of those blubbering kids who couldn't wait for the candy to be doled out at the end of the session.

My throat was dry. The sun hadn't even gone down and I was slurring my words a little because I was drunk. It occurred to me that only one woman was telling the truth. Carmelita or my wife.

"So tell me some of them," Elise said.

"Just," I said, trying to begin. But how do you broach the subject of your wife being a child thief? Or having a half sister? I resolved to start with the bigger secret. Number ninety-nine.

"Just what?"

"How many members are there in your family, exactly?" I finally managed to utter.

"Well, my father and mother are dead," she said. "So that leaves my brother. Who's in a halfway house."

"Is there a half sister?" I said. My voice had a higher pitch than I wanted it to. If there were secrets to excavate, I couldn't start asking them this submissively.

"Half sister?" Elise said. "Is that what she thinks she is?"

"No," I said, startled. "She says your half sister disappeared. Was never heard from again. She used to follow you around like a puppy."

Elise closed her eyes and hit her forehead with the heel of her hand.

"Wait, it's coming to me," she said. "I know it's in there somewhere. Some girl with big brown eyes following me into a forest. Holding my hand. I'm throwing breadcrumbs."

"This isn't funny, Elise. You have to tell me the truth."

"Why do I have to tell you the truth? What will you do if I don't?"

She knew I was powerless, and when she saw how helpless I looked, it seemed to mildly cheer her up for a moment.

"I'm your husband," I said in a weak voice. "Can't you just clue me in a little?"

And there it was: I wasn't even demanding basic respect anymore, just a one-minute head start before everything caved in.

"I'll tell you," Elise said, shaking her finger at me and using a fake drunk slurring voice I hadn't heard in ages, "because I like you, butternuts."

"I'm all ears," I said, glancing through the window at the darkening blue of the sky, the motionless black spines of the scrub pine. The usual platoon of seagulls hovered and drifted along the bay until they became hard to see. Black scraps of paper, floating higher and dipping wildly again.

"My half sister? You know what? I do remember her. One

of my father's great ideas. Forced me to spend the summer with her and her family when he had to go on a business trip. I wanted to kill her the second I saw her stupid, trusting face. This idea that he had another kid and didn't even tell me until about three minutes before he dropped me off. I finally had someone to hate more than myself."

"But she's gone now, right? She vanished. That's what Carmelita said."

"I thought she vanished," Elise said, biting her lip, as if she were keeping a very particular emotion in check. I wasn't sure if it was rage or laughter. "That's what they told me anyway. The girl was a mess. Suicidal. It just had to be teased out."

There it was. The beginning of the end, if you really want to be blunt about it. But my wife didn't show the vaguest tinge of guilt. In fact, it was her face that was reddening as she stared at me.

"And now you just fucked her," she said. "So much for the vanishing part."

Elise watched me twist nervously again on the couch. I guess I'm one of those people who tend to rewind uncomfortable conversations, in the hope that everything eventually makes perfect sense.

"Can we back up a little bit?" I said. "The part where she follows you around like a puppy. How many years ago was this?"

"I was sixteen, maybe seventeen. She was a couple of years younger."

"That girl is more than a couple of years younger than you."

"She wasn't the only girl he made me soften up, Scott. You want to hear about the one who left her mother to get ice cream on a beach? The friend I brought home when I was in middle school? Why aren't they squatting next door?"

I stared out the window again. My favorite time of every

lousy winter day, when the sun set over the marina, its unused yachts tightly shrouded for the winter. I didn't want to think about Elise, wearing a kid's pink sunglasses, waiting in the passenger seat of Victor's sedan as they watched a girl run toward an ice-cream stand to take her place in line. I can see Victor, handing Elise a couple of dollars, saying one or two words of final instruction before she is allowed to push open the heavy car door. A blue day. A perfect glassy sea. A thousand oblivious laughing children.

"You know what?" Elise said, standing up. "We're done."

We were always done. We'd spat out those two words to each other multiple times. But this time, if she just happened to take three steps toward the fireplace, she could pick up the loaded shotgun and aim it at me and she'd never have to threaten me with those words again. I had helped murder her father, and now I was an accessory to all of his old crimes. By the look on Elise's face, I had the firm impression she wasn't going to try to find closure with the ice-cream girl. Or with Carmelita.

She must have seen the uncertainty clouding my face, because she expelled a short jet of air through her nostrils and bit her lower lip. And then it began, her mouth tightening up as she tried to hold back all her emotion. She pawed at her eyes with the back of her index finger, successfully wicking away the moisture, even though her jaw was trembling now.

I was surrendering to my own wife now, slowly raising my hands.

"I just want to understand you better," I said.

"*Understand* me," she said, sneering at me. She seemed grateful to be able to focus her anger outward again. The water in the corner of her eyes dried up. Her lips straightened ominously. I've always been more fearful of her mouth than her eyes in arguments. It always tells me where a situation is headed a few seconds ahead of time. This wasn't a half smile, or even a frown: it was just a dash that looked like it was chipped in stone.

I lowered my arms. I stopped surrendering and stood up. The burning newspaper under the fire had blossomed and burned out, leaving a scant flame on the edge of one of the logs. It needed attending. I got down on my knees, pushed back the grate, and grabbed the box of matches. I could hear Elise passing behind me, and I felt the muscles in my back stiffen. I ripped another sheet of newspaper in two, crumpled it up, and laid it under the blackened log. Elise was climbing the stairs slowly. I knew this because I could see her reflection in the glass of the painting that hung above the fireplace. For a moment, I could see the lower half of her body pause before the top of the steps, her hand gripping the banister, as if she didn't fully trust me alone either. But the shotgun was still leaning against the striped wallpaper, right where she had left it.

I had just struck another match when I heard her shout my name. I leaped up and ran down the entrance hall, took the stairs two at a time. Was there someone in the house? Had she already been taken hostage in Victor's study?

But she was alone, staring into his closet at the open safe.

"She's taken everything," she said. "I don't know how she got the combination."

I touched my wife's stiff arms, which were tightly held against her sides. I was thinking of Victor's last mumbled words to Carmelita. Maybe *Help me* hadn't been the last thing he had said to her. Maybe he'd given her the combination then. Maybe he'd whispered a few last instructions that would put us in more danger than we could even foresee.

"We have everything, Elise," I said, wondering why she couldn't see how lucky we were. "Don't we?"

There was nothing left in the safe besides a manila envelope containing two of Victor's expired passports and a faded green box of Remington UFC handgun ammunition. It was empty.

"He never told you the combo?" I asked Elise, reaching deep inside the safe and finding nothing else.

Elise chucked the worthless passports into the safe and stood there for a moment, looking at the squat iron box, which Victor had spray-painted white on one of his idle bachelor days.

"There was stuff in there no one should see. He liked to keep a record of the things he did," she said.

"He's dead now," I said. "Let the girl keep it if she wants it. Victor can't hurt us now."

Elise squeezed between the desk and the wall, clutching one of the heavier curtains in Victor's room so she could get a clearer view of the house next door. It was early in the evening and it was impossible to make out any shape in the opaque windows.

"He can still hurt us," Elise said. "Forget about the other stuff she's gotten her hands on. She's also armed. He kept a handgun in there. A nine-millimeter he bought from some alcoholic ex-cop who used to work for him."

Elise's cell phone was ringing in the other room. Before she could make a move toward it, I'd already left the room. I was sure it was going to be Curt Page, but when I picked it up I didn't recognize the number.

"Who is this?" I said, staring at Elise in the doorway. She

moved toward me and reached for the phone, but I shook my head and backed away from her.

Whoever it was wasn't speaking. All I could hear was the sound of some faint radio show playing in the background. The muffled voice of some rush-hour DJ discussing an upcoming charity auction in Lancaster. And then the call ended.

"It's probably Curt," Elise said, picking up the phone and glancing halfheartedly at the number.

"That's not Curt's number," I said. "I know, because I called him last night and warned him to stop stalking you."

"You think I know who it is," she said angrily, stuffing the phone into the pocket of her jeans as it began to ring again. "It's some asshole calling the wrong number."

"Then answer it," I said. "Because someone's driving through Lancaster, Pennsylvania, and they sound like they want to talk to you."

She didn't touch the phone. She let it go silent in her side pocket, its blue light still visible through the fabric of her jeans.

"That girl next door could put me in jail for years," she finally said. "And if she does that, I'll take you with me."

"You know what I just realized," I said, though realizing it didn't improve anything one bit. "This is not a healthy relationship."

My wife turned without answering me and I followed her, grudgingly, down the stairs. She paused at the landing, squinting into the sunlight that poured through the front windows of the house.

"What are you waiting for?" I said.

"You need to get the shotgun," she said. "Be careful. I forget if I left the safety on."

We were pretty drunk, I have to admit, when we walked through the pines early that evening, watching the light in the upstairs bedroom of Swain's home extinguish itself. Since we had been using it as a beacon to guide us through the gully on a moonless night, Elise and I had to pause right where we were standing.

"I can't see anything," she said, moving closer to me.

"Upstairs light will come on any second now."

I was carrying the shotgun, but I had been careful to unload it, stuffing the two shells in a pocket of my jeans. The muzzle had quickly turned cold in my left hand, so I blew on it for a moment, then clutched the waxy blue steel.

I hadn't remembered it taking so long for the lights on the timer to complete their nightly circuit. At least thirty seconds had gone by and Swain's house was still completely dark.

"Maybe we should do this early in the morning," I said, shifting my feet and listening to a tiny branch split under my foot.

"So she can see us coming?"

I was going to tell her it was no use when I saw the upstairs light finally switch on. From our vantage point, I could see only the dim outline of Swain's kitchen windows and a hazy whiteness around the sliding glass door. A shadow passed in front of it, temporarily dimming its brightness.

I hadn't even caught a glimpse of Carmelita yet, and I already knew there wasn't a chance I could go through with this. Only an hour ago, I'd sat next to the fire with Elise, watching Victor's newspapers go up in smoke. I'd listened to Elise softly tell me, as if Victor were still breathing in the other room, that we had both made a very serious choice. I did protest at that point, stammering about the spiked Ensure and the fact that the whole fucking thing was supposed to be a fucking rehearsal and that I'd probably never have gone through with it anyway.

Elise had listened to my spluttering cursing fit, her head tilted to one side as if I were one of her speech-therapy clients. And then she stood up, grabbed the shotgun, and told me she was going to take care of it herself. She was about to climb over the fence when I caught up to her and took the gun back.

Now I was just staring at the light in Swain's house, unable to move.

"Scott," Elise whispered. "We can't just stand here."

"I need to run through this one more time," I hissed back.

"There's nothing to run through. You just walk into the house. You keep the gun pointed at her chest."

I cracked open the gun and then I reached into my pocket and fished out the two shells. The shaking had started again. My legs were quivering, my hands, my arms. The jaw again, and I knew it was all fear despite the cold. I couldn't even drop the shells into the barrel of the Browning.

"You've got to help me," I said to Elise, handing them to her. "It's just the cold."

I watched her take them out of my hand and drop them in, each one landing with a faint click. I snapped the gun shut.

It was only about twenty yards to the pool gate, and when we got there we huddled again because we heard a man's voice. It took me a moment to realize that Carmelita must be standing in the kitchen, right above us, playing the old message on the answering machine.

"Swainy," that familiar voice on the machine said. "It's Bill again. You better be dead. Because it's almost September and I still haven't heard from you. This is your last chance to meet us at the Peconic Grill. The oysters are on me."

I couldn't imagine why she was replaying that message, but if she was in the kitchen, I had to move fast.

"Stay here," I told Elise. "I'll shout your name when it's safe."

I reached over, unlatched the pool gate, and ran across the rotting deck, praying I wouldn't fall through and accidentally shoot myself. I made it to the patio, then the sliding glass door, and there was no sign of her. I pulled it open and swung the gun to the right, marching into the kitchen and calling her name.

"Carmelita," I said, bursting into the kitchen just in time to see a figure dash out. The answering machine was rewinding itself, one gray button pushed down. I ran through the same door I had just seen her vanish through, reentering the living room.

I ran after her, but I stopped as soon as I saw what was happening. Carmelita was pointing a black handgun at the sliding glass door, where Elise was standing.

"She never panics," Carmelita said, talking sideways to me as she kept the gun, a nine-millimeter, trained on my wife. For the first time, instead of waiting for the timer, she simply reached over and turned on the lamp in the living room. I kept the shotgun pointed at Carmelita and let her hear me flick the lever of the safety off. The shotgun's polished stock felt too old-fashioned, as if I were holding an antique that would quaintly implode. There was some crosshatching on the grip

I rubbed the back of my thumb against. At least the weight felt good.

"We've all got to settle down," I said. But the words sounded strange and small because my throat had become very dry.

I turned my head quickly to look at my wife, who didn't seem fazed at all that Carmelita was aiming a gun in the general direction of her heart. Elise slowly took a step inside.

"It's freezing out there," she calmly said to the two of us, as if both of us weren't holding weapons. "Do you mind if I close this?"

Neither one of us protested as my wife turned her back and pulled the door shut. Now we were all hermetically sealed in that dusty living room again. I listened to Elise's boot crush one of the fake ficus leaves as she confidently made her way to the fireplace and grabbed one of the iron pokers hanging there. Without warning, she cocked it behind her shoulder and swung as hard as she could, sending crushed bits of glazed tile flying.

"Don't you hate this place, Carm?" she said tauntingly. "Why didn't you leave?"

"Why didn't you?" Carmelita said.

"Victor's dead," Elise said. "He's not going to come back and lock you up anymore. Who's going to treat you like a dog? My submissive husband?"

"He has potential," Carmelita said, carefully keeping the gun pointed at my wife's chest as Elise took two steps toward her. She was wearing Victor's Gore-Tex jacket, its stiff gray fabric rustling in the museum quiet of the room.

"Where's the key?" my wife said. "Give it to me and I'll lock you up right now. We won't feed you for days. You'll never know if we'll even come back."

Something had changed in Carmelita's determined expression. I could see that her hand was trembling, and then her whole arm, to the point where the handgun began to visibly vibrate, as if a train were barreling just underneath the warped floorboards.

Elise took a step closer and had the audacity to touch a black strand of Carmelita's hair, letting it fall through her fingers.

"I know what you like," Elise said. "Don't I?"

"She tied me to a tree," Carmelita said. "When I was a kid."

"Are you going to shoot her right now, Scott?" Elise said. "Or listen to this campfire story?"

"I'm listening."

"Victor drove up with Elise and said he had to drop her off," Carmelita said. "My mom begged him to stay a few nights before he left."

"Her mom was a real loser," Elise said. "Real low-wattage."

Carmelita lifted up the gun again and pressed the muzzle to my wife's temple.

"Say something else about her," Carmelita said. "You'll be dead before you get to the end of the sentence."

Elise thought about this carefully. Her skin had turned whiter and I could see that she was breathing faster.

"I was jealous, C," Elise finally said. "At least your mom was still alive."

Carmelita lowered the gun again and took a step back from my wife.

"She pretended it was a game," Carmelita said. "There was a ball of twine and she tied me to an oak tree and when I couldn't move an inch she told me she was going to set me on fire. That's one of the hundred secrets I was going to tell you."

"Maybe you could just email us a list," Elise said. "Save us a little time."

"I could hear everyone laughing when it got dark. And then I saw them walking toward me along the pasture fence. She was guiding her father by the hand. And then she stood there and watched."

"Watched what?" I said, turning toward Elise. Hadn't they both been there?

"It was pathetic," Elise said, her neck turning red. "The little sounds she made, before he even touched her."

The shot was fired so suddenly, I didn't immediately know what it was. It sounded more like a large book had fallen to the floor than something fatal. But Carmelita had missed by a yard. A dime-sized hole winked at me from the sliding glass door and she seemed just as transfixed by it as I was. *Thank God for her trembling hand,* I thought, watching her shakily raise the gun to Elise's face.

My wife brought the iron poker down toward her skull without mercy. At the last instant, Carmelita moved toward me and the heavy iron hook slammed against her shoulder. I could hear the sound of her collarbone breaking and then saw it protrude from, but not break, the surface of her skin. I had the insane urge to touch it and try to push it back, make everything okay.

"Christ, Elise," I said, but my wife was already swinging the iron through the air again, catching all of Carmelita's wrist and sending the handgun flying through the air. It landed underneath the liquor cabinet, but Carmelita made no attempt to retrieve it. She was crouched near the foot of the staircase, touching her jutting collarbone. It seemed to move away from her fingers underneath her skin, and then it popped up again underneath the collar of her sweatshirt.

"It's broken," she said to Elise, as if her assailant had nothing to do with the awful situation.

I kept the gun pointed at my wife. I felt it was the only thing keeping her from again attacking Carmelita, whose hands were now gripping the wooden rungs of the banister. I could hear the squeak her hands made as she made a tighter fist. It was as if the whole house was about to spin into space and she was grabbing hold of something before it all disintegrated.

"We're going to work this out," I said, growing a little more confident. "Like grown adults. The bad guy is gone. The asshole. There's plenty of money to go around."

Happiness dead ahead. Share a little bit of the wealth. Let's be friends. I was jumping at each cliché, almost giddy now. For the first time in a year, a tangible moment of grace and forgiveness seemed possible, and I would lead us to that place. I could see it, like a sun-struck clearing in some woods. All I had to do was get two victimized women to believe that there was a way out of this. We didn't even have to wind up being wonderful additions to planet earth, but just willing to realize that a dead man had set a terrible chain of events into motion, long ago. There, it was right there on the tip of my tongue.

"Point of no return," I said, taken aback by how hard it was to give the most important speech of my life. I had become oddly stiff and formal again. The man who grimaces as the guests clink their glasses and wait for his speech. "This night has a good ending. You know, for once, I can feel it in my bones. We're going to surprise ourselves tonight."

"Shoot her," a voice said. I was so tied up in my own thoughts that I thought I had just imagined it. But then Carmelita quietly said it again, looking at me imploringly. She must have realized this wouldn't be enough, so she took a deep breath and skipped all the secrets I'd never hear until she got to the best one.

"You want to hear the ugliest secret," Carmelita said. She wasn't trembling at all. This was a better weapon. Lighter than air, one always kept in the chamber.

I was turning toward her, eager to hear what she would say, when I saw Elise leap. She brought the black iron down toward Carmelita's skull again. At the last instant, Carmelita covered her head with her hand and screamed. A tiny wooden chip found my left eye, and I stepped back as the two women went out of focus. My eyes were slathered with their own stinging water now. I wiped them with the back of my hand, and when I could see again, I saw that Carmelita had pushed my wife to the floor and was stabbing at her face with a key she'd pulled from her pocket. She held it as tightly as she could in her hand and went after my wife's eyes, even as Elise violently twisted her head from side to side. I pulled Carmelita backward by her hair and she scrambled to her feet again.

Even though it was for only a moment, Elise looked dazed, two small gashes on her forehead quickly welling up with blood. I watched a sudden arc of spit land on her face and then I saw Carmelita kick her in the head. Her sneaker made a dull slapping sound as it connected with my wife's cheekbone.

I fell on top of Elise like the Good Samaritan I never was, still holding the shotgun with my left hand.

"Put it in her mouth," Carmelita said. "I'll pull the trigger."

But when I lifted up the gun, it was Carmelita I was aiming at. First her chest, and then her back as she walked unsteadily toward the sliding glass door, and then she was on the patio, her blood left on the white handle.

"We can't let her go," Elise said.

I walked past my wife without saying a word, following Carmelita onto the flagstones. Her left hand was pressed against her collarbone again, as if she were pledging some strange allegiance. For a few seconds, before she moved out of the light cast on the stones, I could see how much pain she was in, her mouth curled downward. The faces injured children make when they're waiting for an adult to comfort them. She stood still for a moment, and then, hearing the distant throttle of a truck on 27, turned and started to walk that way.

"He married her," Carmelita said softly. "He actually gave her his dead wife's ring and she wore it all summer. Or maybe she stole it."

The shock of her injury had made her dizzy and she lost her balance for a moment. I caught her just before her knee hit the frozen ground, and she righted herself again. I knew that Elise was right behind me and was carefully listening to everything the girl said. I was terrified that if I said something too sympathetic my wife might bludgeon me next. Even after all the violence that had happened, when I spoke my voice sounded detached, as if I were reading from a transcript Elise might approve of.

"I want to hear all about this," I said. "But it's freezing out here. Let's go back inside the house."

"Ask her where she keeps the ring. I bet she never threw it away. Her dead mother's ring. Ask her about her mother."

But her voice was trailing off now, as if she realized her survival was more important than wasting the ugliest secrets on me.

I followed her around the far corner of the house, past the shrouded BBQ grill that Swain had once used, and then onto the gravel of the driveway, the fibrous branches of a willow tree clacking in the wind. She waited there, only a foot from me, waiting for another sound from the highway. Was it a minute or two minutes that we waited there, the ocean fizzling restlessly behind us, some distant airplane blinking over the house? Elise, I know, was sobbing. I could hear her behind me.

The next sound was just a passing car, nothing more than that, its headlights now visible over the wooden fence that separated Swain's property from the highway.

"I need your help, Scott," Carmelita said. "I'm in so much pain. I can feel the bone moving in my shoulder."

"You've got to come back to the house," I said. "You can't leave now."

She looked at me as if I were crazy, and then, realizing I meant it, stopped in her tracks, just as I had asked her to.

"Good girl," Elise said, just a foot behind me now.

For another second, maybe two, Carmelita considered this vicious compliment, and then she began to walk away again, taking two tentative steps in the gravel of the driveway, then a third.

I raised the gun and pulled the trigger, just before she took the fourth step.

There was an old wooden bulkhead that sat beneath Swain's property. Elise and I dragged Carmelita to the edge of the overgrown lawn and then let her roll down the hill toward the water. Then we walked across the gully and grabbed a flashlight and shovel from the shed under Victor's deck.

Elise and I hardly said a word to each other as we made our way back to the bulkhead, walking along the bay. When I saw the lights from Swain's living room on the bluff above me, I ducked into the gap in the wrecked wall and painted the underbrush and sand with the flashlight until the beam found her hand, her arm twisted behind her back. I stopped there. I didn't want to see what the blast had done to the back of her head. Handing Elise the flashlight, I began digging into the sand, listening to the distant sound of a boat's engine.

Turning off the flashlight, Elise stood by me and we waited until we couldn't see the red and green running lights of the fishing boat slowly making its way to the inlet.

"Maybe this isn't the best place," Elise said, flicking the flashlight back on and cupping it with her hand. She pointed it down at the hole as I shoveled out more sand. I hit a long tree root and whacked it in half with the edge of the shovel.

"Too late to take her anywhere else," I said numbly.

I leaned over the shovel and tossed another clump of sand aside, focusing all my attention on the hole. The only thing I'd buried in my life up to then was a parakeet, adorning its tiny mound with intricately arranged pebbles.

By the time we'd pulled Carmelita into the hole and covered her with sand and seaweed and dead branches, I thought the sky was turning paler.

"You've got her blood on your cheek," Elise said softly, pointing the flashlight at my face one more time. I nodded, too tired to offer my thoughts about this particular issue. I watched myself walk down to the edge of the water, where small waves barely flopped onto the sucking sand. I watched myself kneel down and cup my hands in the bay, lifting its stinking water to my skin, again and again. Over the inlet, like suspended flecks of dark blue inside a marble, the clouds on the horizon became distinct. Elise was already walking back to Victor's with the shovel in her hand, turning toward me and violently waving at me to join her.

It was at the end of that same month, January, that Elise and I allowed ourselves one brief weekend in Miami, unable to relax for one moment. Conspicuously pale and exhausted, we ordered one round of mai tais from the pool bar and then abandoned them by our deck chairs. We spent most of the time on our concrete balcony, trying to read the paperbacks we had picked up at the Hudson News at LaGuardia.

"Do you want to go for a walk?" I said, staring at the tinted windows of the high-rise condo across from us. It had started to rain, but neither of us moved. Inside our room, a football game was playing on the flat-screen television, but I'd already forgot who the two teams were.

Elise was wearing a gauzy silk wrap, her feet kicked up on another chair. Although she still stared down at her Harlan Coben thriller, I knew she'd been stuck on the same page for half an hour.

"What if the water reaches her body?" Elise finally said. "Won't it loosen the sand? Maybe someone passes by and sees some fabric. Or that stupid dog . . ."

"What do you suggest we do about it? Fly back tonight and start hacking her to pieces?"

The word *hacking* made me feel funny. Sick to my stomach, actually. I wasn't going to dig up Carmelita under any condition. How much had she decomposed underneath the sand? What kind of winter larvae were feeding on her? Her corpse would be bloated now, the skin stretched blue and black in places.

"Someone's going to find her," Elise said, finally closing the paperback and tossing it on the ground. "The sooner we deal with it, the better."

The rain had become steadier now, but after months spent on freezing Shinnecock Bay, the warmth of the heavy drops didn't bother me at all. I stood up and leaned over the balcony, where I could see a sliver of the harbor through the buildings. Two WaveRunners sped past, two rooster tails of water arcing behind them. I was so tired that my shoulders ached, and yet it had been impossible to sleep for more than a few minutes at a time. The only consolation had been that when I turned over on my side and faced Elise, her eyes had been open too.

But now, when I turned toward her and gently suggested that we go inside, she didn't move at all. I took a step in her direction, raised her sunglasses and saw that her eyes were closed, her mouth parted, the rain rolling down her forehead and cheek. I bent over her and gave her a kiss on the top of her head.

I was on the verge of wrapping my arms around her, with the idea of gallantly carrying her into the room so she could finally get some rest, when I had a flashback of what it felt like to carry Carmelita's body toward the edge of Swain's property. It's true what they say about dead weight being so much heavier. She kept on slipping through my arms, as if she somehow had some last idea about escaping. I reached under her armpits again and again and held her as tightly as I could, looking for the best place to let her roll down to the sea.

"Elise," I said, looking down at her. "Let's wake up, okay?"

I watched her stir for a moment, then change position in the chair, letting her head fall slowly onto her other shoulder.

Inside the room, her cell phone was ringing. I picked it up and stared at the 347 area code, then I answered the call.

"Merry Christmas," the voice on the other end said. "Is my sister there?"

"It's almost February," I said. "But thanks."

It was the first time I'd spoken to Ryder, and considering I was his brother-in-law, and the fact we'd exchanged exactly zero words up to that point, I thought I might ask him a few questions. The first one was the most important. Was he still in jail?

"No, sir," he said with an ironic politeness. "I am a free man. Overcome with the possibilities of the unconfined day."

"I'd love to meet you someday," I said.

"I'd love to meet *you,*" he said, smashing back my hollow pleasantry. "Shake your hand for putting up with that dying prick. Buy you a beer at least."

"Beer sounds great," I said, noticing the steadier drops of rain falling on the concrete balcony. Elise was awake now. She stood up and arched her shoulder back, only gradually realizing I was on her cell phone.

"I'm going to have to let you go," he said. "I have a thing or two to say to my sister."

"Yeah," I said, already irritated by the way he'd manhandled the conversation. "Merry Christmas too, Ryder."

I handed the phone to Elise, but she didn't even come inside the living room. Whatever it was he was telling her was important enough that she let the rain drench her body. Behind the closed sliding door, I watched a liquid streak of lightning fork on the horizon. Drops of water rolled off her chin and she turned away again as she realized I had begun to try to read her lips.

■

We cut the Miami trip short, of course, and spent a fortune changing the flight. I guess I shouldn't have given it a second thought, considering we had cashed out 112,000 of Victor's preferred Hensu shares, worth a little over twelve bucks each. But we had yet to experience a single moment of joy. In the week since we had "protected ourselves," as Elise put it, we found it harder and harder to sleep each night. In small ways we had become intensely paranoid.

It was Elise though who really started to lose it first. As we were standing in line before security, she had become increasingly agitated.

"Do you think it's weird I'm wearing this cardigan?" she said, plucking at the dark sweater and looking at me imploringly.

"It's just the TSA," I said softly, giving her a sideways hug. "They just want you to walk through their little X-ray peepshow machine."

"I should take it off," she said, starting to tug it off one arm. "It's freezing in here. Isn't it? Is it just me?"

"Yeah, the air-conditioning is turned up pretty high," I lied. The truth was I was wearing only a T-shirt and there was already a sheen of perspiration on my face. I watched Elise roll up her sweater and stuff it in her carry-on.

"I'm good," she said, flipping back her bangs with a finger and giving me a quick smile.

But she wasn't. The line curled around the rope chain two more times and I noticed that Elise was staring at a particular woman standing a few feet ahead of us. The woman had a plain white face and light brown hair. She might have been in her late forties or early fifties. The problem was that she was staring right back at Elise, then me, without the vaguest hint of an expression. Her lips stayed pressed in a tight, flat line.

That was enough for Elise. She whispered something to me I couldn't even hear, then ducked under the rope. I did the same, catching up to her at the freakishly bright counter of an Auntie Anne's.

"I'll take the pretzel nuggets," Elise said, glancing at me. "You want to share them or are you going to want your own?"

"I'll have two of yours," I said, giving the counterperson a patient smile. "My wife's a little bit of a mess. Family funeral."

The counterperson offered his condolences, but I could feel Elise's eyes glued on me as we moved our little red tray down the counter and paid.

She waited until we had taken a seat, and then she lashed into me.

"Don't ever fucking do that again," she hissed at me. "You never make one more joke about any of this. Do you hear me?"

I let her think she'd won that one. Dipping a pretzel nugget in mustard sauce, I leaned back in the chair and chewed it thoughtfully.

"That's going to require an apology," I said.

"Or what?"

"I don't know," I said, squinting at a bland watercolor of some empty golf course at dawn on the wall. "I have to think about it."

My warning, barely a threat at all, seemed to empty all the color from my wife's face. Intently, she watched me pop the second pretzel nugget in my mouth, the way a scientist might study an injected rabbit at Plum Island.

"Scott," she said as I continued to analyze the golf-course watercolor. It looked like heaven to me. I imagined myself purring up to the green in a golf cart, the bracing chill in the air, a family of amiable wild parrots watching me high up in some palm tree.

"Yeah," I said. "I'm still here."

She reached for my hand and pulled it toward her stomach earnestly.

"I'm sorry, okay? I'm completely freaked out."

All the anxiousness had vanished from her face. The fluorescent lights revealed the darkness of the circles under her eyes. Her nails were bitten down to the cuticles. She wasn't wearing any makeup. And despite how humid it was inside the airport, she had to hug herself again, to keep from shivering.

The counterperson, a tall black man with a receding stubble of hair around his temple, approached our table with a basket of fresh cinnamon pretzel nuggets.

"On me," he said kindly. "Looks like you two lovebirds are having a rough time."

When we landed at LaGuardia, we retrieved the Volvo from long-term parking and drove back to Park Slope. A few inches of snow had fallen the night before and was still visible atop the median as we sped down Grand Central Parkway.

We parked the car and walked up President Street and climbed the two flights of narrow, buckled stairs to the one-bedroom we had sublet to a friend of Elise's for the last five months. The key, as promised, was under the mat. Elise had told Michaela that we'd be stopping by to grab some of the photo equipment I'd been storing in one of the closets.

It was unnerving walking into our old apartment, our old life, and seeing how completely Michaela had made it her own. It was tidier than ever before, with a new two-gallon Brita filter sitting on the kitchen counter and one of those collage family photos sitting on our bedroom dresser. Michaela, with the same identical smile, cheek to cheek with everyone she loved. I was looking at it, more than a little resentfully, when I saw Elise cross behind me and flop onto our old bed.

"She's going to be home in a couple of hours," I said, but Elise was already asleep. Her mouth open and a thin line of spit descending onto Michaela's freshly puffed-up pillow.

On the couch, as promised, Michaela had been collecting our mail. It sat in two heaps, bound with rubber bands. I sat down and started throwing out the junk—credit-card offers and auto-insurance quotes. There were a few bills I needed to keep, and I set them aside. Then there was a brown envelope addressed to me, taped up so thoroughly I had to cut it open. Inside, a plastic DVD jewel box and an untitled disc inside.

I gently closed the door of the bedroom and walked into the living room. I slipped the disc into the DVD player. The screen turned from blue to black, but no image appeared. Then suddenly, staring at me with that same condescending smile, was Victor himself. He was standing outside Swain's home in a tan windbreaker, his white hair tossed by a gust of wind. It looked like it might be late summer, just before he was admitted to the hospital.

"Beautiful summer day, isn't it?" he asks, wincing into the wind as if he were standing on the prow of a yacht. The cameraman takes a few steps backward, and more of Victor comes into focus. There are fresh drops of blood on his windbreaker, just beneath the neat little snap-on epaulet. Then he turns and walks back across the cracked paving stones of Swain's patio, the cameraman's dark shape briefly reflected in the sliding glass door, and then the sound changes as they walk inside. It's crystal quiet, quiet enough to hear a woman's voice, instantly familiar, repeating Victor's name.

Victor stops at the small bar, not to pour himself a drink but to fastidiously adjust the cap of the bottle of crème de menthe. Then, followed by the camera, he enters the downstairs bedroom, where Carmelita lies on the bed.

She is barely conscious, her face covered with blood. The window shade has been pulled and the dim light in the room makes it even more revolting to watch. As the camera moves closer to her face, Victor's hand brushes in and out of frame, as if he were introducing an object he had made. But the light is all wrong, and all that can really be seen are the whites of Carmelita's eyes. The rest of her battered face streams away in undifferentiated pixels, as if it were running downstream.

"You're a champ," Victor says, bending over her and yelling into her ear, as if she'd gone temporarily deaf from the blows. The sound of his voice makes her raise her head slightly, but it doesn't bring her back to full consciousness. "Isn't she a fucking champ?"

He's staring at the camera now and his voice has changed and turned deeper and hoarser.

"What do you want to do?" he says to the camera. "You want me to hit her again?"

He raises his palm into the air, right above Carmelita's head, and makes a sudden fist.

The bedroom door opened and Elise stood watching me, her mouth dropping open in amazement.

"Where did you find that?" she said.

"It was in the mail on the couch. Addressed to me."

She tried to grab the remote from my hand, but I pushed her away.

"Michaela just texted me," she said in a distant voice, watching the scene on the video unfold. "She's on her way home."

I was transfixed by Victor's image as he leaned over Carmelita's bruised body. The person with the camera walked around the bed for a better shot. Victor licks the top of her dark nipple and then pushes her left breast back with his hand and bites her hard, just underneath. Carmelita screams so loudly it redlines the audio, making it sound more like high-pitched static.

Elise grabbed my shoulder, trying to get to the remote again, but I twisted away from her. I stood in between her and the television, determined to see the rest of it.

"Turn it off," Elise screamed at me.

Victor, strangely, stares at us through the screen, as if he could hear his daughter's voice. He's actually smiling, and the person with the camera momentarily pans down to his crotch, where he's massaging himself through his khakis.

"Why don't you get on the bed too?" he says to the person behind the camera. "You can lie next to her, like the old days. I promise I won't touch you."

"Fuck you," Elise, the cameraman, says, keeping his momentarily disappointed face square in the frame.

"Do you hear that, C?" he says, turning toward the bed again. Carmelita is pulling a pillow toward herself and for a moment I think she's going to hug it for some false sense of comfort. But she lies on her back, arches upward, and places it underneath the small of her back. With the other hand she drags her panties down her left thigh, too weak to complete the task.

"There you go, Champ," he says, helping her tug her panties the rest of the way off. I brace myself for the next part and quickly look at Elise. She only stares blankly at the screen, with a look of such detachment I want to wring her neck.

"Don't worry," she says. "Nothing more happens. It's like he loses heart. Can you imagine that?"

I watch as Victor takes a step toward the bed and then seems to grow unsteady on his feet. He places his palm on his forehead and sweeps the thin white remains of his hair back.

Then he takes a step toward the camera and dry-heaves twice. He bends over and presses his hands on his knees, waiting for the moment to pass.

"Getting too old for this, Dad?" Elise says to him in the video.

"Shut it off," he says, slicing the air with his hand and then returning his palm toward his bent leg. "Shut it off and lock her up in the closet. We took her out too early. That's what happens when I listen to you and start feeling sorry for her."

21

After plucking the orange parking ticket from the windshield wiper of the Volvo, I warmed up the car. I drove in silence up the Belt Parkway, watching an airplane's wing flash in the sky as it banked toward JFK.

"Why did you help him?" I said.

"Because I always did, ever since I was a little girl."

"And then what you do . . ." I said, incredulous. "Is *stop*. Just stop what you're doing."

"Like we're stopping?"

What was I going to say? That it was all her fault? That I didn't understand exactly how this added up?

"Why did she let him do it?" I said.

"You already know," Elise said, the side of her head touching the passenger window.

"His money?"

"Sure," Elise said, without conviction.

"Or fucked-up sex?"

"Maybe."

"Well, which one was it? I need to know."

"It's me. I'm the one who could have warned her. Because it all happened to me first. You know those poor shits who kneel next to each other in front of a ditch with their hands tied behind their backs, waiting to be shot? They never speak to each other because there's nothing left to say. But I could have changed her life. I guess she had a problem getting over that."

"So she just showed up?"

"I don't know when she showed up last summer. All I knew is that he wanted my help with her, like he always did. Stupid bitch."

"She's your fucking sister, Elise. You could give her that much credit, now that she's dead."

"Half sister. Half slut. Half worthless. Half crazy."

There was a gas station on the median just before Southern State Parkway. I veered off and parked next to one of the pumps.

"Take it slow, Scott," Elise said, reaching toward my knee as I turned off the car. A relentless beeping sound ensued. It didn't bother me.

"Don't touch me," I said. "Ever, ever again, you evil cunt."

She let me finish the sentence and then she reached back and slapped me across the jaw. I suppose I wanted to sit there, waiting for the hot mark left by her outspread fingers to fade. But I turned and I slapped her back, or tried to. I caught mostly armrest as she ducked and then flung open the passenger door.

I dragged her back in by her hair, almost pleased by how firmly it was connected to her skull. I wasn't counting on a Ford Ram truck pulling up right behind me as she kicked wildly, her sneaker thunking against the window. Her scream instantly got the attention of the driver, who raced around my side of the car and pulled open my door.

"We're married," I said helpfully, Elise's black hair still stretched in my right hand, her fist flying into my stomach.

"Let go of your wife," the man said calmly, placing his thick white fingers around my neck until I could feel my eyes puffing out of their sockets. "Or I'm going to start hurting you."

I had trouble with this proposition. I've always had problems with direct threats, no matter who they come from. It's not whether I'm capable of retaliating in any meaningful manner, it's just that I freeze. I'm always waiting for people to come to the conclusion that they're the true idiot, but if there's one thing I've learned it's that they'll keep on increasing the pressure, digging their rebar-strength fingers deeper into your neck.

My Adam's apple felt like it was caught between his index finger and thumb. I could feel the cold metal of his wedding band. He grabbed my other hand, the one that was still attached to Elise's hair, and pinched down expertly on a pressure point on my wrist, automatically snapping my fingers open.

"I've got a confession," I gargled. "You can be the first to hear it."

It was satisfying to feel Elise's heart beating faster. I couldn't see it or hear it, but I knew it was.

"Let him go," she begged this Good Samaritan. "It's my fault. He just found out I was cheating on him."

"You sure about that?" he said. He relaxed his grip just enough that I was finally able to swallow the spit caught in my mouth.

"I'm a moron," Elise said, cupping her hand over the stranger's and gently prying his index finger away. The rest of his hand followed, dropping away from my neck. "I should've waited for a better time."

There were other customers gathered around the car now, peering in at me, shouting offers of assistance to the fat-knuckled Good Samaritan. He patted me insincerely on the shoulder blade, a little peeved that he'd never get the chance to beat me senseless in front of my wife.

"What you're going to do now, guy," he said, offering me one last piece of advice, "is drive nice and safe all the way home."

He reached over and turned on my radio, turning up the volume on a syrupy Katy Perry song.

"I'll be right behind you for a while. Make sure everything is on the straight and narrow."

I love you," Elise said as I cruised up the highway at a steady sixty-eight miles an hour, the Dodge Ram right on my bumper. I did take the liberty of switching off Hot 97, however.

"I love you too, honeybunches," I said robotically, massaging the flesh back to life around my neck. "This is definitely one of those times that being married to you makes absolute sense to me."

She actually had the nerve to put her hand on my right thigh as I drove, running it up and down my jeans a little and bringing her face closer to me. Strange that after all the surreal events of the past few weeks, her breath still smelled kind of nice, her hand felt warm and good, and something was still rattling around my overmatched brain, still wanting to trust her.

I wouldn't let it.

"We're going to have to figure this thing out. This divorce."

"Yeah, that's fine," she said, taking her hand away. She leaned back in her seat and gave our new friend a little wave as he sped by, leaving us alone forever. "If that's what you want to do, then we'll do it."

"And I don't give a fuck about the money," I said. "That's yours. You deserve every filthy little penny."

"It's a lot of money," she said, pressing her finger against the condensation on the passenger window and drawing a little face with *X*'s in the eyes. "You're going to need some of it to get on your feet again."

I thought about arguing that point as well, but then I thought about another Asian bride, posing for me in Prospect Park, another week of making four hundred and fifty, tops.

"Yeah," I said. "That'd be great. Maybe a few months' rent in Albany, or wherever I end up."

We drove in silence past all the ugly-sounding towns on the Southern State Parkway. Ronkonkoma. Shirley. Mastic. We were near Port Jefferson when Elise's cell phone vibrated in the purse between her feet.

"Ryder?" I said.

"No," she said, picking up the phone. She let it ring until the voicemail picked up. But I wasn't going to leave it at that.

"Let me hear the message," I said.

She sighed, quickly punched the code for her voicemail, and then put it on speaker.

"Hi, Elise. You want to hear something fucked up? Your husband left three threatening messages on my voicemail. His voice gets deeper and deeper with each one. Dude is serious. One serious dude. Listen, I need you to remind him that I still have that .357 Magnum and that I'm carrying it right now. I'm also freshly divorced and I'm on the edge. The edge of the edge."

There was a pompous exhalation of breath, and then Curt continued: "I've been driving all night and I just saw the most fucked-up thing. A car just exploded in flames on Interstate 81. They'd set up flares and were waving us through the one open lane. But the driver was burned to a fucking crisp. His hair was still smoking . . ."

"Heard enough?" Elise said. "He probably hasn't slept in days."

"The rest of the family," Curt Page continued, but not before another lungful of air had been expelled to let us know how deep this was going to be. "His wife and kid. They were sitting in the grass nearby. Not a mark on them. That's a story. That's a story I'm going to write just for you, except I'm going to make it beautiful. Tell Scott that. Ask him if he can make the most fucked-up things beautiful like I can."

Curt was so high with interstate insomnia that he forgot to turn off the phone. I could hear the white noise of the highway behind him, the sound of him singing some unintelligible song he'd made up to himself.

All I could make out were the words *golden* and *creatures* and *hot coffee* before the voicemail mercifully cut him off.

"How the fuck did you ever decide I was your type of guy, Elise?" I said. "Why'd you ever single me out?"

She let my question hang in the air for a while, absent-mindedly swiping the face of her phone.

"I thought you were normal," she said.

We made it back to Victor's house late that afternoon, greeted by an agitation of large black crows launching themselves from the scrub pine around the property. A handful of newspapers, in their blue plastic sacks, had started to pile up at the end of the driveway. I gathered them in my arms and walked back into the kitchen, dumping them all in the wastebasket.

Elise was standing out on the deck, scanning Swain's house with a pair of Victor's old binoculars. Then she turned her attention to the bay, panning the binoculars toward the inlet where the radio beacon pulsed against a yellowish sunset.

At least this is it, I thought to myself. I'd spend a few days helping Elise get the house in order, as we'd agreed. A couple of real estate agents were already scheduled to take a look at the place on the weekend. The plan was to be very low-key and stick to the story that had been completely true, up to a point. We had left our jobs in Brooklyn to care for her sick father. Thank God he didn't suffer. What was the market for a house in Shinnecock Hills? We owned two of them.

"Scott," Elise said suddenly.

I turned to see where she was pointing her binoculars. The upstairs bedroom light in Swain's house had come on.

"Calm down," I said, though my throat felt instantly dry. "They just haven't cut the power yet."

"It just startled me, that's all."

I took the binoculars from her and pulled the window into the tightest focus I could. The only thing that had changed was that the wallpaper was now hanging downward from the ceiling, casting its own triangular shadow. I could see part of the dresser and just make out its wooden knobs, and toward the dark hallway a river of that stained white carpet. But that was all.

Zooming in on the other windows, pulling them in and out of focus, I couldn't make out anything in the early-evening light. I was panning toward the upstairs window again when the light suddenly clicked off.

"Did you see that?" Elise said.

"Yeah," I said. "That's the end of it probably. No more power."

Except it wasn't. One by one, the lights in each room came on. Kitchen. Living room. Guest bedroom. Even the chandelier, which I could see the top of. It was as if some mind-fucking phantom had run around the house flipping every switch it could get its hands on. The house was blazing with light now, and I pressed my eyes hard against the binoculars, twisting the focus knob as I searched every visible room.

There was nobody there. Just carpet, and wallpaper, and countertop, and the same old chairs gathered in the breakfast nook. I could even see the silhouette of that four-foot-high pig in the chef's hat and its gleaming snout. THE BEST IS YET TO COME.

"Someone messed with the timer," I said. "Maybe Swain's caretaker comes by once a year."

"There's no caretaker," Elise said. "We're the only ones who care about that place."

We stood there a few minutes longer, bracing for what might come next.

"Maybe it was her," I said. "Maybe she changed the setting right before she died."

Elise wasn't interested in my theory. She stormed back inside the living room and walked upstairs. Even before she reappeared two minutes later, I knew she'd have the shotgun in her hands.

"Let's get this over with tonight," she whispered through the screen.

"They're both dead," I shouted back at her. "It *is* over with."

"We're just unplugging the timer, Scott," she said patiently. "Last thing we need is this little light show every night."

As we made our way across the gully in the darkness, Elise marked the trunk of each pine with a flashlight so I could find my way. It was late January and a few scraps of snow still remained from a snowstorm we had missed. I held the shotgun, as I had the last time, and broke it open, to make sure it was loaded.

"No shells," I said, turning toward Elise so she could see the empty breech.

"Do you want to go back and get them?" she said, flashing the light in my eyes.

I told her to forget it. We'd just unplug the timer and leave Swain's house for good. Of all the things we'd done in the last month, this would be the easiest.

I unlatched the gate to the pool and scrambled toward the patio, with Elise right behind me.

At least everything looked the same. That depressing fake ficus and its ragged circle of dead leaves. It occurred to me only then that Carmelita, bored out of her mind in the winter cold, must have pulled them off, one by one, as she stared at the bay. The only difference I could see was the amount of light pouring out of Swain's house. Every piece of furniture stood in the same position.

I pulled open the sliding glass door and turned toward Elise, who hauled it shut with two hands, its runner sticking in the rust. The skin of her face and neck was flushed, as if she'd just sprinted a hundred yards. She looked nothing like the person I'd met almost ten years before. If you'd held up the two pictures of the now and then, it wouldn't have made any sense. In 2003, she'd been standing on the balcony of a mutual friend's home, with a plastic glass of champagne in her hand. Our first conversation began only vaguely flirtatiously. We guessed each other's professions and got them completely wrong. She had me pegged as a bartender at a fancy steakhouse and I told her that she was finishing her residency at Lenox Hill.

We followed each other through rooms that weren't ours, finally making out self-consciously next to a bed piled high with coats.

And here we were, as we had always been, following each other through other people's rooms again. Except now her eyes darted all around me, searching for something particular. Her black hair was tangled and greasy, and she stretched her hands outward, as if something violent would come hurtling toward her at any second.

"It's probably upstairs," I said.

"What?" she said, briefly allowing me her full attention again. Her pupils dilated as they adjusted to the spot on the living room floor I was standing on. Two feet away from the bar. Eight feet away from the stairs. Right under the chandelier and its hundreds of crystal facets.

"The timer," I said. Now I was the one who felt I should calm her down.

"I heard something," she said. "Did you hear that? Outside."

I told her I didn't hear anything, which was true. It was a windless night. The bay was calm. Through the dark shapes of the scrub pine I could see some moonlight on the frigid water, and the beacon of the radio tower, reassuringly pulsing.

"Take the gun and stand right here," I said. "I'll be right back."

I handed her the shotgun, but its heaviness in her arms didn't seem to make her feel any better. It didn't matter. She could handle the emptiness of that room for a minute as I climbed the stairs, two at a time.

It was odd how the timer had been reset. The lamps in four different rooms had been preset, instead of the lights in the upstairs bedroom that had routinely clicked off around 11:00 p.m.

I was kneeling in the upstairs bedroom, my hand firmly grasping the cheap-looking device, when I heard Elise scream.

I pulled out the whole timer and everything went black, or kind of black, the redness of the vanished light still sliding across my eyes.

"She's here," Elise shouted. Her voice sounded as if it were dropping away.

I was standing at the balcony now, the plastic timer gripped in my hand like some kind of plastic heart.

"Who's here?" I said, trying to adjust to the darkness. I could just make out Elise's legs, but the rest of her body was cut off by the chandelier, its glass barely reflecting the moonlight.

"Outside," Elise called up to me. "I saw her face."

"Carmelita?"

Elise didn't respond. She had taken cover behind the couch, crouched there with the shotgun. I repeated my question as I slowly made my way down the stairs.

"Yes, Carmelita," Elise said. "I'm sure it was her."

I was crouched next to Elise now, safe behind the couch, and I didn't know which was worse: a wife who believed we were being hunted by a ghost or the idea of Carmelita, bandaged and sutured and armed, running around this wrecked house.

"You're sure you saw something?"

"The back of her head. She was running away. She was wearing a man's coat."

This was completely impossible, and I reached for Elise's arm, as if my fingers rubbing up and down her taut forearm could bring her back to reality.

She shrugged me off, ducked her head behind the couch again, the shotgun pointed up at the chandelier.

"Let's go see," I said.

I stood up, leaving my wife hunched there like a refugee, and walked over to the coffee table, where she'd left the flashlight.

I pulled open the sliding glass door and walked calmly up the chipped patio, the toes of my sneakers hitting the weedy tufts between the stones. At the top of the ruined wooden steps that led down to the bay, I stopped and turned around. Elise had followed me to the edge of Swain's property, still holding the gun.

"You're going to break your neck," she said. "The steps end halfway down."

"It's all right," I said, pointing the flashlight up at her. "I'm just going to make sure we're okay."

The steps, just as Elise had promised, did end halfway down. I perched on the last one and clicked off the flashlight. I could see my breath now, faintly, in the quarter moonlight. I could see the outline of black nets that curled around two long poles about two hundred yards offshore. Once I had spent an hour watching a fisherman in a rowboat leaning on each stake, making sure they were still firmly planted in the silty bottom. There was a moment when his body seemed to angle too far off the side of his boat. His hands still gripped the wood and I was sure he'd fall into the water. Part of me wanted to see him fall, expert that he was. I'd even run down the thin strip of beach and offer help, but it never came to that. He simply pushed away and sat down in the boat again, his task accomplished.

Up above me, I heard Elise talking to someone. She was speaking so softly that I couldn't hear the words. What was it that she was repeating, again and again? Was it a prayer? And if so, was she praying for herself, or me, or both of us? Was she asking forgiveness of Carmelita's coat-wearing ghost?

The more I listened to the cadence of her words, the

more I felt it was forgiveness she was after. And then I heard the sound of the shotgun being broken open. A few seconds passed and it was snapped closed again. Nothing closes as perfectly as that. If it made her feel more brave to let a ghost know she was ready to take her on, then let it be.

Myself, I just poked the beam of the flashlight around the gray sand beneath me. Then I pushed off the last splintered step and jumped, the back of my head bouncing off a half-buried scrub pine root. I held on to a tangle of branches and listened to the sand sluice around me. The sound was almost peaceful, and I tried hard to pretend I was just out here playing a game. The flashlight, beam still intact, rolled down toward the bulkhead and flared out.

I let myself roll down the dune another ten or fifteen feet, my sneakers filled with sand now, a bloody scrape curved across the back of my neck and skull. I picked up the flashlight first, clicked it uselessly on and off, then chucked it angrily toward the water.

I knew where I was, or at least I thought I had a good idea. There had been two tall pine trees just uphill from where we had buried Carmelita. Two pine trees that had grown so close that when the wind picked up, I remember hearing the two trunks creak against each other. This was the sound I had listened to as I finished burying her.

There was no wind now, so there was no creaking. But even in silhouette I was sure it was these two trees.

I got down on my hands and knees and started to dig with my hands. As soon as I felt one rigid limb, one stony finger, I'd shout up to Elise, finally giving her the reassurance she needed.

I scooped out handfuls of hard, cold sand. The small pebbles caught under my nails.

"Is she there?" Elise said. She was standing on the last

step. I could see the blackness of her hair, darker than the rest of her face. When she moved I could see the barrel of the gun.

"Give me a minute," I said. "And be careful with the gun. That whole staircase is ready to fall into the sea."

For some time, I dug in silence, scooping and flinging the sand to my sides. Then I thought I felt Carmelita's arm and it terrified me.

"Got it," I said, my mouth going dry. Because it was an *it*. A hard bony length of arm, gone scaly underneath the sand. But when I pulled, all the sand around it seemed to move, and when I ran my hand down its length I realized it was just another buried scrub pine root.

"Is it her?" Elise said.

"No. Just a root. Maybe I'm in the wrong place."

Above us, I could hear the distinct sound of tires on Dick Swain's driveway. It was odd enough that I immediately stopped digging and looked up at Elise.

"You hear that?" I said.

She didn't say anything, which infuriated me. Had she been immobilized by fear again? Did she think Carmelita was driving up to the house in a brand-new car?

"I don't hear anything," Elise finally said.

I could hear it. The driver turned off the engine. Whoever it was climbed out and slammed the car door.

"Please keep on digging, Scott," Elise said. "You have to find her."

I stood up. I was done with digging, and I was just about to let her know that when I heard a man's terse voice call her name. *Fucking Curt,* I thought. *He's found her.*

"Keep digging, Scott," Elise said.

They were standing together now, Elise and Curt. I heard him whisper something to her, to which she mumbled something I also couldn't hear.

"Hey, Curt?" I yelled up at him. "Why don't you read me some of that story you wrote for my wife? Or some of that unpublished novel that we always laughed about behind your back?"

"That's a grand idea," Curt said.

Except it wasn't his voice. And there wasn't any pretentious *haaaaah* of air after the statement. No, it positively was not Curt Page, and the moment I realized it I felt more fear than relief.

I'm not stupid. I'm not the sharpest tack in the drawer, but I've always managed to piece together my small moments of doom, up till now, and done my best to avoid sailing into them head-on.

There was nothing in the cold sand, and then there she was. A piece of hard fabric. The softer texture of shoelaces. An empty sneaker. All that they'd left of her. She'd been moved, of course. And I'd be killed here. Then moved.

Elise's friend, whoever he was, had taken the gun from her. I could hear him whispering something important to her now, almost as if he were asking her for a cue, and I knew the barrel was trained on me.

My wife didn't say anything. My wife was an absence. Elise, her name always reminded me of the word *ellipsis*, and the tiny dots that replace the dreadful secret. Suddenly, she simply wasn't there. It was only when I heard the thump of her foot against one of the upper steps that I realized she had left me for good.

"That's good," he said. He had no discernible accent. His voice just sounded tired. As if he'd worked two shifts and then busted his ass to get down here and finish one last job. "Use her shoe. That way you'll get more sand."

I knew who this was now, but I didn't permit myself confirmation just yet. Because that was the only person, besides me, who'd believe he had so little to lose that he'd do anything she'd ask.

I did as I was told. I knew if I stood up and ran one step in any direction he'd blow a hole in my back anyway.

I dug like a child in that sand with Carmelita's sneaker. I scooped out tar and pebbles and something wormy with its heel until I realized the rubber had been eaten through.

"Merry Christmas, Scott," Ryder said.

I was about to answer him, because I thought we had left it that he was going to buy me a beer. I was about to tell him how nice it was to finally meet him in person, when he pulled the trigger.

There was a moment in which I thought I was saved. I was only lying on my back and looking at what was left of the moon. Maybe *it* was what had been shot away. There was music playing on the car radio now. Elise didn't want to hear what was happening down here, and when I opened my mouth to point this out, I swallowed my own blood, and what was left of my front teeth.

This is her story, I wanted to tell him, arching my back a little so I could begin. Blow away the rest of the moon. Not me. Because I could be the best friend you ever had. I could save you a whole lot of trouble right here, right now.

He was standing over me now. I think he was. I think I was still holding Carmelita's sad little sneaker, squeezing it as if it could bring me some last good luck. In the distance, Elise was getting impatient. She'd hit scan, and the radio was only touching on songs. Five seconds on each one. It landed on something ridiculously smooth and jazzy. *Please don't let me die on something jazzy,* I thought.

Give me five more seconds.

Blood was pooling around my head now, cooling instantly in the sand. It was hard to believe it was mine.

I thought it might be time to picture that tree in Prospect Park. The one that burst into yellow flame a few weeks before every other one. The one where I liked to take all my shy brides.

I'm lifting my camera to my eye again and it's the bride by herself this time, doing just what I say, her husband patiently waiting for his turn, hands clasped and head bowed as if he were attending his own funeral.

Acknowledgments

I'm humbled that I had the good fortune to work with my editor, Robert Bloom, and my agent, David Gernert, and that they believed in this novel.